THE SINISTRA ZONE

ÁDÁM BODOR

Translated from the Hungarian by Paul Olchváry

A NEW DIRECTIONS BOOK

Grateful acknowledgment to the Hungarian Cultural Fund,
which supported the translation of this book.

 *Nemzeti
Kulturális
Alap*

 *National
Cultural Fund
of Hungary*

Copyright © 1992 by Ádám Bodor
Translation copyright © 2013 by Paul Olchváry

Originally published as *Sinistra Körzet* by Magvető Könyvkiadó in 1992 and published
by arrangement with Acontilado, Barcelona.

Manufactured in the United States of America
First published as a New Directions Paperbook (NDP1255) in 2013
New Directions Books are printed on acid-free paper.
Design by Erik Rieselbach

Library of Congress Cataloging-in-Publication Data
Bodor, Ádám.
[Sinistra körzet. English]
The sinistra zone / Ádám Bodor ; translated from the Hungarian by Paul
Olchváry.
pages cm
ISBN 978-0-8112-1978-5 (alk. paper)
1. Totalitarianism—Fiction. I. Olchváry, Paul. II. Title.
 PH3213.B518S5613 2013
 894'.511334—dc23
                    2012050353

10 9 8 7 6 5 4 3 2 1

New Directions Books are published for James Laughlin
by New Directions Publishing Corporation
80 Eighth Avenue, New York 10011

THE SINISTRA ZONE

1

COLONEL BORCAN'S UMBRELLA

Two weeks before he died, Colonel Borcan took me with him on reconnaissance to one of the barren heights in the Dobrin forest district. He asked me to keep my eyes open, especially on the mountain ash trees, whose clusters of little red berries stood out in the roadside scrub, to see if the waxwings had yet arrived. It was mid-autumn, and the brush was abuzz with unfamiliar sounds.

Such patrols by the forest commissioner began with a visit each morning to the bear reserve, where he sized things up. On the way home—while ambling along some mountain ridge, breathing in the intoxicating silence of the preserve, and perking his ears to the babbling brooks in the valleys below—he would formulate a report on what he had seen. Now, though, making his way along all but impassable trails by following markers left by the mountain infantrymen, he was headed straight for a secret lookout. Word had it that the waxwings had indeed arrived, and in their wake so too had the fever that visited this forested region each winter and that, in the Sinistra Zone, was for some odd reason called the Tungusic Flu.

An open rest area of sorts constructed out of lichen-splotched rocks and padded with moss awaited Colonel Borcan at the summit. On reaching it he dropped his leather umbrella, the sort used by the mountain infantry, on the grass nearby. Then he loosened his greatcoat and found a comfortable spot to sit down. He removed his cap, too, anchoring it under on a few rocks. Bareheaded, his hair fluttering in the wind and his ear-lobes turning red, he sat there for hours on end, eyes glued to binoculars he trained on the eastern horizon.

This secret vista—a crag that jutted out slightly beyond the spruces and firs—formed a rocky part of the crest of Pop Ivan Mountain. From it you could see far across the border to the bluish, rolling, forested hills of Ruthenia. Dark smoke rose from behind the furthest hills, perhaps from as far away as the open country beyond. As if night were already coming on, a purplish curtain draped the horizon to the east, but it faded with the rising sun.

When, hours later, the valley filled with the opalescent lights of afternoon, the forest commissioner packed away his binoculars and picked up his hat: the reconnaissance had come to an end.

Whether he had in fact caught a glimpse of what he sought on the slopes across the way—of the waxwing or some other sign of the Tungusic Flu approaching from bush to bush—this was to forever remain his secret; nor did I ever figure out why he had taken me—a simple harvester of wild fruits, and a stranger at that—along to the Ukrainian border that day.

On the way home, once we were down in the valley, he asked if I'd seen a waxwing. "I did," I replied, "two, maybe three," whereupon Colonel Borcan announced he would put in an order for inoculations.

We were already near the barracks when the colonel—the only mountain infantryman who roamed those dank forests both summer and winter with an umbrella under his arm—once again dropped that umbrella on the grass and removed the binoculars from their case; for it so happened that the stranger whom folks around there called the Red Rooster was at that very moment walking along the edge of the blanched autumn hayfield beyond the stream.

Feet hardly touching the ground, the Red Rooster moved along the ridge of turf that marked the border between forest and field; his red hair and beard blazed against the black of the spruces and firs. Through his binoculars Colonel Borcan followed him until the Red Rooster disappeared into a lustrous yellow swarm of birch leaves. Then he spoke to me, in a hushed, almost intimate tone.

"Andrei, you sure you didn't get a little package for me, by mistake?" He must have gathered from my confused stare that I barely understood what he'd said, for he added, "Just a freshly caught fish?"

Although the question was odd, as was his bereft expression when I replied that I had no package for him, I would no doubt have forgotten the episode entirely—except that not long after that, the Red Rooster called on me at the fruit depot, with a fogged-up plastic bag swinging from his hand: in a little water, glistening at the bottom, was a fish. This bag and its contents would rightly have been the forest commissioner's. By that time, however, Colonel Borcan was no longer alive.

Most residents of the Sinistra Zone have dark brown or black hair. Blondes are awfully rare; redheads, nonexistent—with one exception: Bebe Tescovina, the commissary manager's little girl. Everyone around there knew Bebe for her orange-red hair, shining from afar like mountain ash berries. Since the locals weren't in the habit of dyeing their hair, whenever another redhead chanced to turn up, everyone knew at once, even from a distance, that it could only be a stranger passing through.

The Red Rooster seemed to be an idle wanderer. As he cut

across the slopes with those easy steps of his, his hair and beard would suddenly glimmer against the blackness of the spruces and firs like a rosebush full of luminescent red hips. It was midautumn when he arrived, and the rosehips were in fact ripening under the bite of early frosts. One morning, tracks left behind by foreign-made rubber boots appeared on those frosty trails. His boots.

He was a slight, wispy fellow who spoke Ukrainian, Romanian, Hungarian, and even Carpathian German. But he spoke none of these well. The Red Rooster probably didn't have a decent command of a single language spoken around here. Even his way of walking, a self-assured swagger, wasn't the way the locals walk. Besides, he seemed to spend all his time outside, as if to leave no doubt in anyone who might see him that the only reason he was rambling along the Sinistra River was to gaze in awe at the mist-shrouded mountaintops.

In the vicinity of Dobrin, where this stranger paid his respects almost every day, the Sinistra branched off into various smaller streams, and steep valleys cut deeply down the ascending face of Pop Ivan Mountain. Winding their way along water-worn ravines up to the mountain's rocky ridge were barbed-wire-wrapped steel rods, concrete posts, and watchtowers: the gullies were laid with traps. The border ran along this watershed ridge. The thick web of fences, ditches, and various other obstacles opened at just one crack in a drafty mountain pass: only from there did the old dirt road go somersaulting into the hills beyond, bathed in the foreign lights of the north.

At that point a blue-and-yellow crossing gate blocked the road, and a tiny guardhouse stood beside an old canvas tent full of shivering soldiers. Although this was the only operating border post in the Sinistra Zone, the gate was lifted just once a week, for a few hours every Thursday morning. The soldiers on patrol marked the occasion by nosing about each other's side of the border for a bit in the spirit of military brotherhood, and the two or three civilian vehicles with a permit from the regional authorities to travel this route would then cross over.

The Red Rambler, as he was also called—whose hair, dress, and slapdash posture gave him away as a foreigner even at a distance—did not show up for the first time on a Thursday, but on a Saturday. Masons dismantling the forest chapel happened upon his tracks one morning; and hours later, Géza Kökény, a night watchman who spent his insomniac days in a watchtower at the edge of the village, spotted the redheaded stranger descending the slopes of Pop Ivan Mountain. He seemed to move as easily as the wind about the barbed-wire-tangled brush. Down below, he was asked more than once for his papers, but the infantrymen found his I.D. in order even if it was, after all, presumably forged.

He wore brown rubber boots and a gray felt jacket of the sort worn on the far side of Pop Ivan Mountain—a jacket with patches of green corduroy. His narrow-brimmed hat, ornamented with kestrel feathers, dangled on his back from a long cord. Fluttering from the top of his head was that crest of red hair, and a rakish beard, parted down the middle, decorated his chin.

From the start, on glimpsing this stranger, Géza Kökény dubbed him the Red Rooster. And sure enough, since no one knew his real name, this simple but exact nickname stuck.

A dappled calfskin satchel adorned with brass clasps and fittings hung from the man's shoulder, and a semitransparent plastic bag swung from his right hand. Wriggling about inside, like a silver-bellied fish, was a shiny platter. Sometimes he would approach the locals working in the forests or fields and offer it for sale, though surely he must have known that they hadn't any use for platters. For a while everyone was guessing about just what, in fact, the fellow was up to: prying about, getting a sense of shopping preferences in these parts, was he? Out to determine just how friendly the locals were? The mountain infantrymen hassled him for a day and a half, asking repeatedly for his papers. But then, it seems, they were told to let up: from then on they hardly gave him a second look. Besides, nobody so flamboyant, however he tried, could possibly make it as a spy.

Each and every morning, the lower reaches of forest were tinged a pearly gray with hoarfrost or sheathed by a film of passing nighttime snow, so the regular trail of footprints from Pop Ivan Mountain toward Dobrin was visible even from a distance on those downy hills. Sometimes a whole flock of waxwings—which make their appearance in the Sinistra valleys from the north, as a harbinger of winter's numbing winds—accompanied the stranger in his wanderings. Meandering over on those blanched fields with the birds swirling above his head, this redheaded stranger seemed not to have come from the Ukraine at all, but straight out of an old picture book.

Waxwings, by the way, were not too well liked around there. Most locals chased them away with stones, and clever folks just spat at them—it was believed that where these birds flocked, the Tungusic Flu would be follow in short order—the very fever that, in the end, did in Colonel Borcan.

The colonel, poor fellow, looked me up again—something he didn't do too often—only days before his death. Practically begging, he grilled me one more time about that package.

"Come on, Andrei, tell me the truth. Didn't someone leave a plastic bag for me at your place? With a fish inside, that's all. It's okay if you ate it, but at least tell me."

Although I swore up and down that nothing had come, the colonel left with a brooding look of suspicion and resentment. We never met again. Before long, Nikifor Tescovina, the commissary manager in the conservation area, spread the news that the forest commissioner had disappeared. All the bear wardens and colonels frequented the commissary, so he knew all there was to know.

And it was indeed Nikifor Tescovina who soon announced that Colonel Borcan had been found, dead as a doornail, on a bare mountaintop. A bird had already built a nest in the colonel's gaping mouth. Later, someone—a poacher dressed in a mountain infantry uniform, no doubt—nailed the corpse to the ground, thrusting bayonets through the hands and clamping the feet between the rocks, so as to keep the griffins from tearing away his flesh.

Not long after that, the Red Rooster looked me up at what was then my workplace, the wild fruit depot. There I coordinated the harvesting of not only fruit—blueberries and blackberries—but also mushrooms. Actually, I lived there too, in the storage building, amid the scent of fermenting fruit emanating from so many tubs, buckets, and barrels.

I recall that incident perfectly, because on that same day a new harvester, Elvira Spiridon, stopped by to drop off a load of berries. I suppose there's no harm in adding that Elvira—the wife of Severin Spiridon, who lived up in the mountains—would later become my lover. In any case, that day she introduced herself with a large basket of blackberries and a satchel full of parasol mushrooms.

A few hundred bears were kept in the Dobrin conservation area, and since they were partial to blackberries and parasol mushrooms, we delivered these from the fruit depot I oversaw.

As I couldn't help but notice, this woman—a trembling, fidgety tendril, a fiery snake, and a red-hot titmouse all at once—was suddenly limping dramatically. That got me thinking: if only a thorn were to pierce the sole of that foot, why then it would be my job to remove it. Well, it may have been a ridiculous wish, but Heaven heard it. While I emptied the basket of blackberries into a barrel and spread the mushroom caps about on a sieve, Elvira Spiridon sat on my threshold and, to my delight, with the bronze loops of her enormous earrings flashing about, she set about wrestling with the sandal strap around her ankle. I didn't hesitate a bit. I knelt down before her, placed her foot in my lap, and unwrapped the white felt rag she used for a sock. Her stubby little foot was still tan from gathering in the hay that summer, and a purple web of veins filigreed over the surface. Her sole was tender, moist, and practically pink, as if she tiptoed all day. Cutting into it was not a thorn, really, but a thin, tiny, and nonetheless prickly golden-silvery thistle leaf. Naturally I pulled it out with my teeth. Then, after letting it glitter a moment on the tip of my fingernail, I licked it before tucking it under my shirt. Meanwhile I was clutching Elvira Spiridon's foot in my hand. Had someone spotted us just then, he might have understood that I was simply introducing myself to her.

Sure enough, someone really was lounging about nearby. Without so much as a rustle, all at once a silhouette with colored edges appeared on the threshold: the Red Rooster. Could it have been anyone else? The leather satchel's mounts and clasps gleamed blindingly. In his right hand was a plastic bag, and wriggling about in the murky water inside this bag was a silver-bellied fish shaped like an oval platter.

"Andrei," he said, addressing me without further adieu by my first name: "Take this to Colonel Borcan. Before the sun sets."

"Sure," I agreed, embarrassed by the proximity of Elvira Spiridon. "Just put it down over there."

By then Colonel Borcan was no longer alive, but that wasn't any of the Red Rooster's business. I threw the plastic bag, with the fish inside, into an empty barrel, and as soon as the stranger left I hurried after Elvira Spiridon—who, glittering earrings and all, was dashing away in fright into the marshy meadow with one foot still bare, the sandal dangling in her hand. In vain I conjured up one flattering word after another: they flew past her ears to no avail. It seemed she had lost heart on encountering the Red Rooster.

Back then, in any case, I happened to be wooing Aranka Westin. As far as I could tell from subtle cues, the old bag wasn't exactly indifferent to me, and so I got to fantasizing: maybe, just maybe, one night while her boyfriend made his rounds of the barracks, cutting the infantrymen's hair, Aranka would scurry right out of the village in nothing but a flimsy nightshirt or perhaps even stark naked and make her way along the little stream straight to the fruit depot, where I lived all alone. She, too, worked for the mountain infantry, as a seamstress, so apart from such fantasies I would in fact regularly check in on her, sometimes late in the day, on the pretext of frayed collars or dangling buttons.

This is what happened after the Red Rooster's sudden autumn visit: I woke up in the middle of the night to the cackling of wild geese driven toward the Sinistra peaks by the thick clouds of chimney smoke enveloping the open country to the east. The dead silence of such frosty nights was broken regularly by the passing birds, whose stifled calls—not at all unlike the occasional mewlings of the track watchman's clarinet—rattled down chimneys and echoed in ash-laden stoves until the crack of dawn. As on that night, this disquieting sound invariably woke me up, reminding me of my solitude and conjuring up thoughts of Aranka Westin.

Deep inside the village yards, through the latticework of denuded plum tree branches, light still issued from her window. I tore a button off my jacket and, after stealthily climbing over a few fences, before long I was there, tapping on Aranka Westin's window.

She reached out for the jacket. Stitching while I stood there at her window, she asked, "What the hell was that red stranger doing up by you?'

"You mean the Rooster? Oh, I don't even remember—nothing, I think. He only asked if he could use the outhouse."

"Now, now, Andrei, don't you get mixed up in anything. Everyone knows he left a plastic bag with you. I hear there's a silver fish inside, a really nice one."

This irritated me so much that, on getting home, I took the fish, which was still busily writhing in the barrel, to the outhouse at the far end of the yard and dropped it in the hole. I wanted to keep my mouth shut about the whole thing; I had no desire to wind up in some affair that would get me banished from the Sinistra Zone—where I'd gone years earlier after getting wind of the fact that my adopted son, Béla Bundasian, had been exiled to a conservation area there. I'd come here hoping to pick up his trail. It would have been a shame to now let down my guard and ruin everything I'd managed to attain by now; after all, I'd gotten myself appointed Harvest Coordinator.

But something was up. At dawn the following day the Red Rooster came back again. Unkempt, bathed in sweat, his hair matted, and mud-stained up to his thighs, he made his way hastily across the weedy meadow. His hair didn't even look fiery now; but his skin, his ears burned with terror and rage, and his nostrils flared.

"For god's sake, Andrei," he hissed, "Why didn't you tell me Colonel Borcan was dead?"

Why, indeed. I shrugged. *Because.*

He wanted the fish, and as soon as he realized that I hadn't eaten the thing, and knew where it could now be found, he ran off to scoop it out. He then scrubbed it clean in the stream, wrapped it in a burdock leaf, tucked it into his dappled calfskin satchel, and left, disappearing forever from Dobrin.

A new forest commissioner, Izolda Mavrodin, arrived to replace Colonel Borcan as commander of the mountain infantry. My life changed. And one blustery spring day I, too, disappeared from there.

Many years later, a Greek passport in my pocket, I rolled about the roads of the Sinistra Zone in my sparkling new, four-wheel drive, metallic green Suzuki jeep and spent a day, just a day, in Dobrin. I arrived via the Baba Rotunda Pass, figuring I'd take a quick look for my one-time lover, Elvira Spiridon, amid those meadows of thyme; or, more precisely, on the upper floor of the cottage she shared with her husband, Severin Spiridon, in a roadside clearing.

But where their house had once stood lay just a heap of dark blue cinders drenched with rain and ice. Tender young blades of grass, along with fresh sprouts of nettle and saffron, encircled the spot: almost certainly their grave.

It was late afternoon. The eastern horizon was ablaze with clouds of woe: a heavy, orange-red cumulus bank. Lately, such distant passing clouds—creamy, puffy, resplendent towers that faded into the purple veils of night—had been conjuring up the past and making me a bit sad. I left the jeep by the side of the road and, crestfallen, walked along the edge of the forest to a few familiar spots.

Winding through the clearing before me were two tight parallel bands of depressed soil that sparkled in the reflection of the clouds—ice or, it seemed, maybe glass. All at once it hit me that these were my own old ski tracks. Left over from the final winter I'd spent here in the pass, they snaked their way through the incandescent spring grass and, finally, into the darkness of the forest. Anyone who has skied through woods knows how the snow—if you pass over your own tracks several times—gets packed down underneath, sometimes melting just so, then freezing over and over again. Even once such a double set of tracks melts, an impression is left behind, a silky, silvery sheen that fades entirely only by early summer. Sometimes it never does.

•

That last winter I skied every day along the meandering subterranean streams of the Kolinda forest, which break the surface here and there. A few unauthorized recluses had been hiding there from the mountain infantry in dank, underground lairs and caves; no promises or requests could get them to emerge. At first the authorities had me set traps for them; then, in the end, we simply cemented up the cave openings. That's why I skied about this area with sacks of cement on my back, always on the same tracks, for weeks on end. Cement is heavy, mind you, and under my weight the snow had crystallized, like diamonds.

Lost in reveries of my bygone life, I then noticed two parched red wigs hanging from a spruce tree, swinging back and forth in the wind. Skewering them with a twig, I examined the wigs up close: one was a head of hair; the other, judging by its form, was a beard. In a shaded corner of the clearing lay a young man, stretched out on the slimy fallen leaves of spring, snoring loudly in his dreams as flies buzzed all around him. On his side, a mottled calfskin satchel; beside him, an empty bottle, tipped over. He resembled someone I knew. I hurried away.

Now a foreigner, I took a room in the Dobrin Inn after registering my arrival with the authorities. But once darkness fell—and after just a couple of drinks, of course—I sneaked out and spent the night with my onetime girlfriend, Aranka Westin. She was the one who then informed me that Colonel Borcan had been sentenced posthumously to death—it turned out that he and a Polish colonel had been cooking up some scheme, and the Pole had been in the habit of smuggling messages, and sometimes real dollars, across the border to Colonel Borcan in the bellies of fish.

But I didn't want to hear a thing about that affair.

After all, as an essential part of the story, it should also be noted that we didn't let all the time that had passed us by keep us from a little reunion that night, under the cover of darkness. There I was lolling beside her, feeling my pulse, and just beginning to muse about staying near Aranka Westin for at least one more day, when that clarinet-like, caterwauled shrieking from high above us broke the spell: wild geese were announcing their presence in the clouds over Dobrin. As could be heard unmistakably through the silence of the night, they were coming from the south, from the Kolinda forest, and turning overhead suddenly north, toward Pop Ivan Mountain. I felt their calls to the tips of my little fingers. There's not a sound more disquieting than theirs.

So when the mountain infantry came to get me around dawn—stating that since I'd secretly left my designated lodgings, they must revoke my residence permit and ban me forever from the Sinistra Zone—I'd long been wide awake, waiting for morning, waiting to finally be done with the place.

2

ANDREI'S DOG TAG

One spring day I arrived by bicycle at the Baba Rotunda Pass, and it was from there that I first glimpsed the imposing peaks at the foot of which I would later all but forget my life up to that point. In the valley below, the Sinistra river basin reposed before me under the long, sharp shadows and orange light of the afternoon. Willow groves and sparse rows of village houses loomed in the distance along the river bends; shingled roofs glistened on distant, sunbathed slopes; and further yet, the icy peaks of Pop Ivan Mountain and Dobrin shimmered above their thick black collars of spruce and fir. Behind them: the icy green, foreign, northern sky.

There were no more roads from there. The conservation area where I planned to lie low was surely somewhere near, under those steep mountainsides. And deep in that wilderness lived Béla Bundasian, my adopted son. For years I'd been searching for him.

The main road, after winding its way down from the pass, followed the railroad embankment for some distance until all at once the double set of train tracks disappeared into a tunnel. The track watchman stood at the entrance, playing a clarinet.

And then, further down, near the village, the embankment ran up alongside the road once again, and before long the main tracks were joined by a local, narrow-gauge railway line. Bicycling along, I arrived at the terminal of the Sinistra branch railway almost simultaneously with the train.

The tracks came to an end by a ramshackle one-story building. Hanging from its eaves was a wooden board painted with the name of the village: DOBRIN. That wasn't all. Someone had sketched on the wall below with mud: CITY.

It was spring when I arrived in Dobrin City, toward evening.

Having propped my bike up against a railing, I waited for the throng of silent passengers who'd just gotten off the train to pass by. Some wore rubber boots; others, sandals. I figured if someone seemed agreeable, I'd strike up a conversation. This was my first time in Dobrin.

Smoke stirred above the station—wood smoke, for the trains around there ran on timber—and a few clouds even crept upward along the main road, away from the station, as if pulled along by the passengers now walking home. A man with olive-brown skin stood leaning against the wall of a loading platform across the street. Blinking incessantly, he eyed the openings that formed in the departing crowd. He wore a dirty white tank top and stained army trousers; sandals held his bare feet. I had no intention of greeting him, but once the passengers had dispersed, he jumped off the ramp and ran directly over to me across the now empty space.

"You look," he said in a soft, greasy voice, "as if you need a place to stay."

"Well, something like that."

"I know a place."

That is how I met Nikifor Tescovina. His name was obvious from the start: a sheet-metal dog tag dangled on a chain around his neck. For his part, he didn't want to shake hands, much less know my name. "Let's not hurry things," he said. "Just who you are can wait until Colonel Borcan looks you up." He explained that the forest commissioner who commanded Dobrin's mountain infantry would, among other things, decide on a name for me.

"Maybe you haven't noticed, but nobody here rides a bicycle. You won't need yours anymore—just leave it there, someone will take it."

He was always one step ahead of me as we walked through the village, which stretched out across the bottom of the valley. More than once he stepped into a puddle to wash the dust off his sandaled feet, as if summer had arrived, though in fact hardly had the sun disappeared for the day behind the peaks to the west than a cuticle of ice had started to form around all the puddles. A narrow, weasel-shaped patch of snow glistened on the steep mountainside above, and the cut power lines that dangled from the utility poles along the main road in Dobrin City swung back and forth as a cool evening breeze, spiced with the scent of spruce buds, swept down into the village

"Everything here belongs to the mountain infantry," Nikifor Tescovina explained in that same soft, greasy voice. "The place you'll live in, too—they take care of people around here."

"Up to now I've seen them only in pictures," I replied, in as hushed a tone as possible, "but I've heard the mountain infantrymen are decent soldiers."

"Oh yes—and make sure to tell them you lost your papers. Colonel Puiu Borcan will pretend he believes you."

"Oh! My papers—" I said with a start. "I stuffed them under the bicycle seat. I should go back and get them."

"Oh, forget about them—your bike's gone by now, anyway. Forget those papers ever existed."

Toward the end of the village, a stream passed in white torrents under a covered wooden bridge, and beside it sat a dwarf, soaking his feet. Before long Nikifor Tescovina turned off the road into an alley that soon narrowed into a trail. Making its way along a small stream whose soggy banks were overgrown with weeds, this trail passed between the village yards out into a meadow. At the far end of the meadow, beside a cluster of spruces, willows, and black alders, stood a decrepit old building with a dented but glistening roof. It looked as if it used to be a water mill, but the stream had changed course, leaving the mill high and dry on the meadow. Birds nested in the building's broken windows and twilight showered down from the sky through the cracks in the wood-shingle roof like a mass of thin, many-colored, shimmering blades. The mill's axles, grindstones, and other onetime furnishings had long been removed, and the evening scent of the meadow blew gently through gaping holes in the wall.

Nikifor Tescovina passed through a hollow space between those walls and straight up to the second floor and stopped before a wide-open, rickety door. In a corner of the adjacent room, which seemed to have been used to store tools and other things, was a berth of freshly torn spruce branches.

"You can lie low here," said Nikifor Tescovina. "No one's going to ask you a thing."

"How did you know I was coming?"

"Ever since you set foot in the Sinistra Zone, Colonel Borcan has followed your every move. This area attracts people like you—they follow the Sinistra River upstream and don't stop until they reach Dobrin."

"Then the colonel knows I'm just a simple wayfarer, that's good to hear."

"Oh, of course he knows. And what is the simple wayfarer planning to do? You seem versatile."

"Well, I'm at home in the woods—I know about trees, bushes, mushrooms, fruit. I've worked at food markets. I can work at a lumberyard or help peel trees. I could even set traps."

"Sounds good. I'll tell the colonel. But until he comes by, don't leave—In fact, don't even step outside."

"And what should I do if nature calls, in a big way?"

"Just stick your ass out the window."

Nikifor Tescovina waved good-bye by putting a palm to his forehead. By the time he reached the far end of the meadow, where the village fences began, dusk had swallowed him up. Leaning over the windowsill, I kept looking his way until from behind me an owl flew outside, amid a great buffeting of wings.

Days passed before he deigned to show himself again, but every morning I found a little bag hanging on the doorknob, a bottle of water always inside it along with a few congealed boiled potatoes; onions; a handful of prunes; and some hazelnuts. Those days there, spent consuming such fare, fused together as quickly as the fog passing over the meadow; for a long time I had no idea whether it was Monday, Wednesday, or Saturday. The passing of time was signaled by the changing shape of the patches of snow on the mountainside above Dobrin.

One morning, though, there he was again: Nikifor Tescovina, seated on the threshold beside the dangling bag of grub.

"I'm glad to see you've been sleeping so well," he said. "I've stopped by more than a few times but didn't want to wake you. I thought: let the guy get his sleep. In the meantime, though, Colonel Puiu Borcan and I got to talking about you."

"You mean he has time to think about me?"

"Of course he does—he's the forest commissioner, right? He wants to see you—so he'll come by soon. It looks like you can stay here in Dobrin."

"If you've really arranged that, I'll repay you someday. I'd like to make a go of it here. Something tells me this is this is the place I'll make something of my life."

"That could well be. Colonel Borcan figures that if your proposal to oversee wild fruit harvest is serious, something can be worked out. He thinks the harvested fruit could be stored here at the mill in barrels and tubs."

"Exactly my plan."

"And then, in the scent of fermenting fruit, you could sleep and sleep."

"In that case, now I'm really curious to know how the blackberries are around here. I've been thinking mainly about blueberries and blackberries."

"I'm not really sure. The truth is, it all depends on the bears, on what they want. They're the ones who will be eating what you collect. A hundred, maybe a hundred and fifty of them are kept in the preserve: they are why Colonel Borcan liked your idea."

All day long I leaned out the window, waiting for Colonel Borcan to show up, gazing at those mountain peaks that seemed by turns headstrong or capricious. But for weeks on end, only shadows—sometimes of clouds; other times, of flocks of crows—made their way across that meadow that stretched out between the Sinistra River and Dobrin City. Spring rain came from the west, from the Sinistra peaks, and the clouds, colliding with the steep walls of Mount Dobrin, lingered for days around the icy summits. A mass of cottony clouds would sometimes descend from all sides upon the peaks like a veil of plush fabric draped over a sculpture. When it finally lifted days later, there stood Mount Dobrin once more, still glistening white even as below it, spring had taken hold all around. Whenever Nikifor Tescovina arrived toward night with that daily bag of food, we'd sit on the building's lukewarm threshold and breathe in the scent of laurel rising from the stream.

"As you can see," he would reassure me again and again, "you enjoy our complete confidence—no one will ask where you came from, and you won't tell anyone, either. If someone starts badgering you with questions, go ahead and lie."

"All right—I'm sure I'll get into the swing of things. And what the hell, I could always just say something different to everyone."

"That's perfect—you're getting the picture. And as far as your name is concerned, forget it right now. If you hear your name hissed somewhere nearby, don't turn a hair—always a poker face, OK?"

The darkness that enveloped Dobrin after sunset every day was so thick that above the dark contours of the village houses the only light to be glimpsed came from the distant windows of the military base. Sometimes flashes of light shot out in purposeful signals from the mountain infantry's watchtowers as well. And then there were the lightning bolts that might rip through the nighttime clouds up above Mount Dobrin, the faraway accompanying murmur of thunder intermingled with the hooting of the owls from down in the woods. The foggy yellow light of dawn invariably found me leaning out the window.

One day Nikifor Tescovina arrived with his little girl. Even from a distance, the child's short, blazing red hair gleamed through the fog like a cluster of ripe mountain ash berries in the fall. They were near the mill by the time I noticed that the father had his daughter on a leash. A stone's throw from the entrance, he tied her to the tall, yellow post that marked the place, and then he entered the building alone.

That day Nikifor Tescovina brought along a bottle of denatured alcohol as well as a sheet-metal mug and charcoal in a metal pot that had been drilled full of tiny holes. For it to be drinkable, he explained, the alcohol had to be filtered through charcoal into another container. In the absence of charcoal, he said, timber fungus or blueberries would also do the trick.

"It'll make you puke at first, but you get used to it."

"I bet."

He'd already begun to pour the liquid over the charcoal, holding the mug underneath and watching for the first drops.

"Soon you can get to work. The colonel has already ordered up the tubs and the buckets, and he's also hired a team of women to harvest the fruit. They'll swarm around you like honeybees, but watch yourself. Like I said before: no matter what, keep that poker face."

"Lately I've been the soul of self-discipline."

"Good—make sure you keep it up if you run across a fellow named Géza Kökény. He'll tell you that he's famous, that there's a bust of him on the riverbank, but don't you believe him."

"I won't even hear him out."

"That's the spirit. Over there, by the way, is my little girl, Bebe," he said, extending an open palm toward the meadow, where the redheaded youngster tied to the post was now sitting about on the grass. "You'll get to know her. She's just eight, but she wants to leave me already."

"Don't you let her."

"She's fallen in love with Géza Hutira."

"I don't know the name—sounds like an alias."

"Hmm, who knows. He's the meteorologist in the preserve. About your age—fifty, at least, but with his hair down to the ground, and he's got my little girl's heart in his hands."

I'd been holed up in that abandoned water mill with voles, bats, and barn owls keeping me company for four, five, maybe six weeks already when Colonel Puiu Borcan finally looked me up in person. He dropped by with my new name. Winter returned that day for a couple hours to the forests of the Sinistra Zone. An icy mist descended on the blossoming meadow, a shimmering glassy mush formed on the backwater tributary, and mountain clearings shone in all their snowy resplendence over the village below. I glimpsed the two approaching figures through drifting wisps of fog. One of them was my benefactor, Nikifor Tescovina. The other—a baggy-faced, big-eared man in an officer's greatcoat—adjusted his hat on his forehead as he came.

His hand held a big black umbrella. Although icy drops of vapor from the passing storm still permeated the air, his umbrella was closed, its sodden black fabric limp as the wings of a sleeping bat. An enormous pair of binoculars swung from his neck.

This, then, was the forest commissioner, Colonel Puiu Borcan.

Later, once I'd earned his respect, I too had the opportunity to peer through those binoculars. On one occasion I accompanied the colonel way up into the woods, and while he went on alone into a thicket, he entrusted me with them along with his umbrella. It was Revolution Day, so I knew the mountain infantrymen were playing badminton down by the stream with the Dobrin railway workers. To this day I recall how that tiny snow-white birdie kept flashing back and forth above the prairie of swaying virgin grass that was taller than any of the men.

Anyhow, on that first day of our acquaintance Colonel Borcan came to a halt on the threshold, the binoculars about his neck and the umbrella hanging from his hand. His expression was woeful and a bit clammy. Reflected off the distant snowy clearings sunlight was shining right through his earlobes, and on the tufts of hair frizzed out from underneath his hat. The freezing rain had already come and gone that day, but drops still clung to the stubble on his chin.

"So you're the one."

"Yes."

"And what's your name?"

"I don't know—I lost my papers."

"Well, fine, then."

From his pocket he removed a sheet-metal dog tag that dangled, glistening from a watch chain. On it, freshly engraved: ANDREI BODOR. My alias. Colonel Puiu Borcan himself put it around my neck, and then clamped the loose ends of the chain at my nape with little pliers. No sooner had he done so than the metal began warming my skin. *Andrei,* now that part of my new name I especially liked.

3

ARANKA WESTIN'S WINDOW

For weeks, months, maybe years I'd been living in the Sinis-tra Zone under the alias Andrei Bodor when a trackman's job opened up at the narrow-gauge forest railway. Sheet-metal-sheathed freight cars and scrapped mine cars ran along this route hauling fruit, horse carcasses, and other provisions to the bears in the conservation area. There, somewhere inside the fence surrounding the preserve, far from the world, lived my adopted son, Béla Bundasian. It was on account of him that I'd moved to this mountainous area up north to begin with. So as soon as I heard that the trackman Augustin Konnert had been found in several pieces one morning beside the rails, I applied for his post.

Although I probably wasn't the only one who applied, in no time I was summoned to the base for an interview. While waiting in the hallway I met up with the barber of Dobrin, who had just been banished from the Zone. That day marked the beginning of my lifelong friendship with Aranka Westin.

This was around the time that the wild fruit depot in Dobrin had been shut down, and although I had immediately lost my job as harvest manager, I was allowed to stay on in the storage building, sleeping in a small room among the barrels and tubs. The depot was situated in an abandoned water mill on a meadow, along a stream that was in fact a backwater tributary of the Sinistra; this stream had long ago changed course, veering away from the mill during a spring flood—leaving the old stone mill isolated on the meadow in the company of spruces, mountain ash, willows, and black alders. The spot was marked by a tall, yellow-painted post that could be seen from far away even on cloudy days, so the women arriving from nearby mountainsides after harvesting fruit could find their way there even in thick fog.

On the morning of that memorable day, a brown slip of paper torn from a bag fluttered on that now superfluously towering yellow post. On it, in hastily scrawled letters, were these words: *"Andrei, hurry to the office. Serious business."* The message was for me, written by Colonel Coca Mavrodin herself, the new mountain infantry commander in Dobrin. I recognized her handwriting from the backward *n*'s and *s*'s. The unknown messenger must have tacked the note to the post in the early hours—tracks made by rubber boots groped their way about the rimy soil near the post. Autumn was drawing to a close.

Circumventing the trail through the meadow, I flanked the willows along the stream and didn't meet up with a soul except for the bust of Géza Kökény, which appeared through the latticework of denuded tree branches. Dobrin stretched out beyond the stream, and beyond the village, almost on the mountainside itself, stood the mountain infantry barracks, looming gray at the bottom of the precipice like some massive pile of fallen boulders. Further yet, in one of the valleys extending to the border, lived Béla Bundasian, my adopted son.

It's a simple, everyday story, this tale of ours. One fine day Béla Bundasian did not return home from Moldavia, where he went regularly to get sheet music paper from black marketeers, and

I never saw him again. For a week or two after his disappearance, it seemed conceivable that once again he was passing the time with his lover, Cornelia Illafeld, a hot-blooded woman who lived somewhere right in the middle of the Carpathians, near a railway tunnel. But when he hadn't shown up even weeks later, and hadn't sent so much as a sign of life, it was safe to assume he'd gotten mixed up in something or other.

He'd gotten mixed up in something, all right. But only a year and a half later did it become clear that Béla Bundasian had been resettled in the vicinity of the Ukrainian border and was now living in a conservation area within the Sinistra Zone. All this I learned from an anonymous well-wisher—perhaps some local official—by way of a note etched with a needle onto a coin dropped into my mailbox.

Such news is far from a cause for celebration, perhaps, but it elated me nevertheless. I soon gave up my job with the main office at the food market, where I had been working at the time as an inspector and, on occasion, a specialist identifying wild mushrooms. Having done so, I traveled north, hoping to land a job in some mountain village along the Sinistra River. I followed my nose all the while, and finally—years having passed in the meantime—I ended up precisely there, in the vicinity of the conservation area in question: dank, drafty Dobrin City.

Harvesting wild fruit and mushrooms is a sure way of getting by even in the leanest of times, for you can always fill up your own satchel in addition to the government-issue pack basket. Blueberries, blackberries, and chanterelles are, of course, much appreciated by many people. But it wasn't some big canning factory we supplied, just the nearby conservation area: bears were locked up in the ruins of a chapel and caged in abandoned, caved-in mines. Through dropped hints and wily inquiries, I figured out that Béla Bundasian was living in the meteorologist Géza Hutira's cottage—above the timber line, amid snowcapped peaks.

Not that he had anything to do, but as a favor to the meteorologist he would sometimes go outside and note the positions of the weather vanes on the cliffs or take readings from various measuring instruments scattered about the mountainsides. He never did come into the village, so I waited for our paths to cross once again by chance.

As if he had seen right through my plans, the region's previous forest commissioner, Colonel Puiu Borcan, had been unwilling to sign a pass that would have allowed me to harvest on the preserve. But then Puiu Borcan came to an unexpected end, failing to return from one of his patrols. For a while people waited for him to return, figuring that maybe he'd reappear after some drawn-out escapade, but when a solitary black umbrella floated over Dobrin City like some sort of giant bat, carried by the wind—only he, mind you, the commander of the mountain infantry, used such an umbrella on his patrols—everyone knew the colonel was no more.

Colonel Puiu Borcan was succeeded as commander of the mountain infantry in Dobrin by a woman, Izolda Mavrodin, who went by the nickname "Coca." She was a slender creature—quiet, diaphanous, like a dragonfly. Whenever she wanted to see me, she'd send me a note, just a few short words, and ragged at that, invariably torn from a paper bag. What's more, recognizing her messages was easy, and such brown, coal-scrawled strips of paper fluttered even now, as I walked, tied to dry stalks and denuded twigs along the trail that led to the base: "We're waiting for you, Andrei, on very important business."

Coca Mavrodin had summoned others that day to the office as well, and the hall was full of spruce-gum-scented lumberjacks, forest rangers, and the like. So it was that while awaiting my turn, I met up with the barber of Dobrin, Vili Dunka. As if no longer recognizing anyone at all, he was just leaving her office with hurried, disdainful steps. But I went after him—after all, we sometimes got together for a drink or two.

Vili Dunka, however, was no more pleased to see me than anyone else. He was in a hurry, he said, explaining that he had to clear out of the village, in fact, the whole Sinistra Zone, on the first train. That morning he'd been summoned to the base with orders to bring only a traveling bag, a change of underclothes, and his most cherished personal effects: from there he was headed straight for the station. The barbershop had been closed in Dobrin City, as had the bars; all the venues where people had been in the habit of chitchatting or lingering about had been shut down. As if to prove his story, Vili Dunka pulled forth a complimentary train ticket allowing him to travel for free to his designated new abode.

"And what does Aranka Westin have to say about this development?" I asked.

"Nothing. It doesn't apply to her; she'll go on patching up officers' greatcoats. She'll be staying here."

The woman in question was the base's seamstress, and until that day had lived with Vili Dunka.

"I ask because as you know," I said, continuing my initial line of thought, "you'll be away for many years. In fact, you might never come back at all."

"That's how it looks—I'm ready for anything."

"Well, I don't know if you ever noticed, but my mouth has always watered for Aranka Westin. Now that you're leaving, I'll do everything in my power to fill your shoes."

"Yeah, that's crossed my mind. But it's simple: I just won't think about you two."

"I'd like to be up-front—I wouldn't want it to look as if I'm up to no good behind your back. I wouldn't want you to think that."

"For me, you two are history. Most of my things are still there, with her. Take anything you want. My undershirts, slippers, underwear—that's all there, and we're about the same size. All I'm taking with me are scissors, razors, shaving cream and a couple of brushes. My barber's supplies, you know. Everything else is yours."

"That's really decent of you."

"What the hell can I do?"

"Then again, who knows what's going to happen—as you can see, they've called me in here, too."

"But you don't have a bag with you. You can stay. At least for a while."

"I sure hope so—that's why I'm taking the liberty of asking for a few words of advice. How should I behave—what are her habits, her womanish whims?"

"Damn it, man, just concentrate on her big white shanks, not her whims. But all the same, let's just say that if she's busy sewing, don't even think of making a move. With her, duty always comes first. And now I've got to be on my way—all the best."

"Thanks. Take care of yourself, okay?"

With that, Vili Dunka, the former barber of Dobrin, headed off. From the hallway window I watched him make his way past the glistening puddles all over the yard to the porter's gatehouse in the towering concrete wall that surrounded the property. He waited at the booth for an officer to open the gate and let him out. I kept watching as his path on the opposite side of the wall was indicated by sparrows taking flight. Vili Dunka disappeared down the road to the station, and that was the last anyone ever heard of him.

It was late afternoon by the time I was called in for my interview. Seated in the forest commissioner's chair was the coroner, Colonel Titus Tomoioaga. Explaining that Coca Mavrodin was occupied at the moment, he reassured me that she was reviewing my application for the trackman's job. He added that there was, however, a little hitch: my files had been lost while being taken to the records office. Until they turn up, he said, they would solicit personal references about my character from a few trustworthy individuals. And, who knows, even if the track-man's job wasn't possible, Coca Mavrodin might just employ me as a courier of sorts; for someone was needed to take messages into the conservation area.

It seemed they wanted to send me to the very place I'd been banned from until then. After waiting for so many years, perhaps finally I would cross paths once more with Béla Bundasian. Feigning indifference, I conjured up a lackluster expression, as if this was not quite what I'd had in mind. Indeed, after waiting so long for just such a turn of events I couldn't even bring myself to be too happy about the news. Besides which, to be honest, my thoughts were still on Vili Dunka, who sat waiting at the station with that complimentary ticket in his pocket. The sound of a short train-whistle would mean he had left. It would be nice, I thought, to try on his slippers that very night.

Being late autumn, night was already coming on as I left the base and passed along Dobrin City's empty streets, with their vagabond fogs and the barking of dogs. More than a few years had passed since the power lines had been cut, so for the most part the local houses cowered each and every night in muted darkness; even now, early in the evening, hurricane lamps and tallow candles glinted here and there.

A pale window shone faintly like daybreak from deep inside the yard of Aranka Westin.

For a long time I peered through the gaps in the curtain, watching her rummage about in a widowed sort of way, watching her patch up those heavy wool-felt uniforms in the flickering candlelight. A thick wool shawl was draped over her back in a triangle: its tip reached her bottom, its two wings nestled onto those thighs Vili Dunka had called "shanks." No doubt she was a bit cold. It seemed she hadn't had the time to light a fire that day.

I went around the house to the woodshed, bundled a few logs into my arms, grabbed some kindling, then went back around and, without knocking, opened the door by pressing down the handle with my knee. Aranka Westin looked up momentarily, flashing me another quick look or two as I clumsily closed the door, again using my leg. If her eyes were indeed seamstress sharp, she might have noticed the trousers trembling just so around my leg—perhaps, she might have thought, from the draft. At least five years had passed since I'd been with a woman.

I waited for the first encouraging sign: for the furrows to subside on her chin, for her toes to slacken invitingly in her slippers; and, above all, for her to finally drop from her hands the officer's greatcoat she was painstakingly equipping with new pockets of gray felt. This little venture of mine was a sure thing, I knew, and I knew another thing, too: not even by chance should I try anything as long as the sewing went on.

4

COCA MAVRODIN'S NAME

When it was announced that Colonel Puiu Borcan had been found on one of the windswept heights over Dobrin, I shook the dust from my quilted jacket and soaked my muddy rubber boots in the stream. Then I looked up Gábriel Dunka, the dwarf, to have him trim my hair a bit. Colonel Puiu Borcan had been forest commissioner for the Sinistra Zone, so it was only proper that I, who managed the wild fruit depot, should show up at his burial looking decent.

It soon turned out that all the fuss was in vain. The ceremony was not to be: Colonel Izolda Mavrodin, the newly appointed commander of the mountain infantry, had banned all public gatherings well in advance. While still on her way from Dobruja to her new post in this northern mountainous region, she'd sent word that Colonel Puiu Borcan was to stay up there on the mountaintop exactly at the spot where the fever had done him in, and that no one should dare even touch him. Presumably this meant not even if, by chance, badgers or foxes wandering that way were to close in on the colonel's corpse.

So Colonel Borcan was succeeded at the mountain infantry in Dobrin by a woman. It was said that Mavrodin was but an alias, that her real name was Mahmudia, and that she didn't mind being called Coca. Practically no one got any sleep in Dobrin City the night before her arrival, judging from the anxious whispers snaking their way through town. For a while, though, it seemed plausible that what I was hearing was instead the squealing of the track watchman's clarinet by the tunnel or, say, late-migrating wild geese passing over the valley. As I sauntered through the yard in the middle of the night toward the outhouse—the denatured alcohol I downed every evening served to clear my bowels often enough—I noticed a yellowish fog looming in the dark beyond the village's unlit houses. All the lights were on in the barracks, and the watchtower lights looked like huge tufts of cotton candy in the dank night. Screeching sounds also came from the barracks: the mountain infantrymen were no doubt busily polishing the hallway floors with pillows tied to their feet and scrubbing windows with damp newspapers.

Izolda Mavrodin arrived early the next morning in a Red Cross military jeep. Someone had fingered her nickname into the furry white film coating the peak of her cap, as well as onto the vehicle's windshield and its mud flaps: *Coca*. The bitter smell of medicine—or of squashed bugs?—permeated the streets of Dobrin City as the jeep whizzed past. Having surged out in continuous waves as it billowed through the village, this odor collected like rainwater in roadside ditches and in yards.

That very day Coca Mavrodin-Mahmudia selected some fifteen to twenty villagers based on appearance alone; which is to say, they all looked virtually the same: long-necked, goose-headed, button-eyed, colorless youth. She had their frieze coats discarded, whereupon each was given a gray suit, a pair of black oxfords, and a silvery necktie. Locals wasted no time in dubbing their transformed neighbors "the gray ganders." Not that there was time to train them, but they figured out on their own what they were to do; and from the start they proved adept at casting weighty stares at everyone wherever they went. Whenever they headed off somewhere as a team, their leather-soled shoes click-clacked against the wet pavement.

Wasting no time in making an introductory visit to pay my respects, I soon found myself standing before the new forest commissioner in my now dustless quilted jacket, my rinsed and freshly shined rubber boots.

But before she'd even finished looking me over, which she did thoroughly, she ordered me to leave her office.

In the days and weeks to come she left me messages here and there, scribbled little trifles. But whenever I then reported to her in person, out of breath, she would send me away once again. "Must be some mistake," she'd say, claiming to not even know who I was, while at other times she'd say: "Let's put that off for now, we'll talk some other time." I had no doubt she wanted only to test me, to get on my nerves, and that one day she would be ready to reveal her true intentions—whether openly or not. And then she would have her mountain infantrymen, her dogs, and her falcons search under every rock until I turned up.

I may have been getting on in years, but that didn't stop me from flirting madly enough that fall with Aranka Westin, and not without cause for hope. When, as sometimes happened, she would be left unattended after a delivery, I'd go look her up. One fine morning the gray ganders found me there engaged in some serious kissing. Hardly had they arrived, and they were already taking me away.

The next stop was the office of Coca Mavrodin, who now announced that she'd been grappling long and hard with the question of what should become of me. The wild fruit depot had been shut down, she noted, and so my post as harvest co-ordinator had ceased. Since I hadn't been born around here, anyway, but who knows where, it would be best if I soon left the Zone altogether.

"Strawberry picking, mushrooming, rambling in the woods—that sort of thing has seen its day," said Coca Mavrodin in a subdued, colorless voice. "In fact, it's been completely unnecessary for some time now." After a pause she added, "But the biggest problem is that your papers are missing. You can't stay here."

To drive home her point, she now pulled a worn-looking gray file folder from her desk that bore the words ANDREI and BODOR in big, scrawled letters. My alias. She opened it up and showed me, as if to indicate that I didn't exist, that it was empty. It couldn't be ruled out, she said, that someone or other, figuring my papers were not needed, had burned them or thrown them out—or maybe the documents had self-destructed.

By jingling the sheet-metal dog tag that hung from my neck, I now showed her that Colonel Puiu Borcan had had me registered in the usual manner, so that if need be I could prove my identity. Those in Dobrin who worked in the woods wore such dog tags engraved with all of their personal data. Around here, that was what counted as real identification.

"If you were to stay here," said Coca Mavrodin, "you'd need that one day. But now you won't, as long as you're alive and kicking."

Short, hunched, and pallid, Coca Mavrodin-Mahmudia was buried deep in her greatcoat like some lurid nocturnal moth. Even her eyes were leathery: they didn't so much as blink. And yet—as the stink of dead bugs steamed from her lusterless, felt-like hair and from the yellow tufts of cotton in her ears—her black nostrils flared at me.

"All the same," I said, figuring it was worth a try, "if possible I'd like to stay, anyway. I'll do anything. I've already applied for a job as signalman with the narrow-gauge railroad. Maybe we can still talk things over."

"I've heard of your plans," said the forest commissioner with a dismissive wave of her hand. "But once the snow falls, that rail line shuts down, and I'm not so sure I'll be starting it up again come spring. Sooner or later you'd get into trouble here—come on, you don't even have a name. Get out while you can, with your honor intact. Go while I let you."

Her words were clear enough, so I took hold of my cap, cast her one or two malicious glances instead of a greeting, and spit out the open window on my way to the door. Coca Mavrodin's voice reached me on the threshold.

"Stop right there. Go ahead and spit, I don't care—but I thought you were a gentleman."

"I am, and besides, I didn't spit."

"That's different. Then I can ask you for a favor, after all. There's a pass around here, The Baba Rotunda Pass. I'd like you to guide me there. I'm not exactly crazy about having these mountain infantrymen take me." She turned around, chair and all, raising a finger to the topographic map on the wall. Searching out the high point where the main road began to somersault back downhill on the other side of the range, she added, "To be honest, I've never spent much time in this sort of terrain—I'm from down south. So it would be a relief if a civilian would show me the way, someone I won't be seeing again in any case."

"All right. I won't refuse."

The gray ganders sat beside each other on a bench by the entrance, sweat gathering in white welts on their black oxfords. Their button eyes sparkled in the bright autumn sunshine and the smell of cheap cologne.

"This here," said Coca Mavrodin, pointing at me, "is the big bad bird. He's promised to leave. Tomorrow morning you're to accompany him to the border of the Zone. Wait there till he takes wing and flies away."

The Red Cross jeep was waiting in front of the barracks. The rainwater swaying about in a tiny puddle on its canvas roof was speckled with blue, leeching from the fallen birch leaves that floated on top; this puddle also held a crow—a crow with upturned feet. In those days, birds would often drop right out of the sky.

Géza Kökény, the valiant bear-keeper of old, was basking in the sun at the front gate, puffing his Pope. As the smoke reached me, my nostrils caught the aroma of languishing thyme. In a salute of sorts he raised the fingers of his right hand to his forehead.

Winding its way up to the Baba Rotunda Pass in eight or nine zigzags was an old dirt road pockmarked with sparkling puddles and slashed here and there by water-filled ditches. Except for a single bus route that led toward Bukovina, it was used only by charcoal burners, forest rangers, and the mountain infantrymen of Dobrin. At the top, in addition to a few tiny farms scattered about some clearings, was the home of road worker Zoltán Marmorstein: a log cabin faded gray from wind and rain. There we stood facing the steep rock walls of Dobrin; the Kolinda forest loomed to the east, and the crags of Pop Ivan Mountain blazed weasel-red to the north.

This, then, was a sort of get-acquainted session, an initial joint reconnaissance mission. I went on ahead of Coca Mavrodin, bending back the branches to clear the way for her, kicking spruce cones off the path and clapping loudly to scare away the birds in plenty of time. A week or two earlier the mountain ash trees still held their clusters of fiery red berries, but by now only denuded branches remained: the waxwings, which feed on the berries, had arrived, driven here by the piercing winds up north.

To break the silence, I mentioned this bit of natural history trivia. At first Coca Mavrodin seemed not to notice. Only minutes later did she reply.

"So you're a man of learning—I still don't have any use for you," she said. "A man shouldn't give his mind over to fruit and birds. What the hell grows around here, anyway?"

"Blueberries and blackberries were my specialty," I replied.

"As you know, I delivered supplies to the nature reserve. The bears are partial to blackberries."

"I've never seen a blueberry in my life, but you'll show me one, all right? As for blackberries, we've got the trailing sort down in Dobruja, dewberries. We don't get much snow, but all year round the hills and knolls are white with salt, and the dewberries trail all over those pale mounds, with their furry stems packed full of leering little berries."

"Must be interesting."

I wasn't exactly in the mood for polite conversation. In fact I was terribly annoyed at being forced to leave. The couple of years I'd spent in the Sinistra Zone suddenly seemed in vain. I had hoped to help my adopted son flee once I found him; or, if he didn't want to go, I would have taken Aranka Westin with me. And now along came this woman, Izolda Mahmudia, to banish me. I huffed and I puffed, spitting furiously.

"Say, Andrei, you don't happen to have any idea what might have become of your papers, do you?"

"Yes I do," I answered peevishly, "I believe they stayed in the big man's pocket."

"What big man's?"

"In *his,* of course—the Colonel's." Lackadaisically I pointed ahead to the snow-covered peaks above Dobrin sparkling amid ragged drooping clouds: there Colonel Puiu Borcan rested on a lone mountaintop in eternal peace among flat green stones.

"That's too bad. Don't even think of rummaging through his pockets. They say he was done in by the contagion. I'm going to have a fire lit under him. And don't call him 'The Colonel' anymore."

Minutes later, flying low over a distant rolling meadow and bouncing repeatedly off its hillocks, came Colonel Puiu Borcan's umbrella. In no time it had flitted on, passing right by the rock walls above Dobrin.

"I've never in my life seen such a big bat," whispered Coca Mavrodin.

Past a spruce-covered bend along the road, beyond road worker Zoltán Marmorstein's cabin, stood an alpine farmhouse; near this farmhouse was a barn, a hay shack, and a tiny wooden shed. Glistening black heaps of manure steamed on the rimy autumn meadow along the fence. Severin Spiridon, a mountain resident recognizable on sight, ambled along among the piles with pocketed hands, sometimes looking up in apparent alarm. Huge black birds, carrion crows, strutted along on the ground before him; a woolly, dappled dog followed behind.

Having been the first to notice the manure piles, the dog, its tail erect and swaying in the wind, promptly urinated in spurts. Severin Spiridon stopped, too, a hand half covering his eyes as he peered into the distance through the translucent wisps of steam rising from the manure. First he opened his jacket at the neck, then his trousers, and keeping one hand above his eyes, he, too, nervously relieved himself.

"Who's that?" asked Coca Mavrodin.

"Severin Spiridon—You'll meet him, Miss, he's been with the mountain infantry for a while now."

"Just between us, I don't care for these mountain infantry-men. Each and every one of them is a cocky little bastard."

Severin Spiridon had meanwhile circled his house and was now peering about with a pair of binoculars that he must have found hanging somewhere or other, for they hadn't been on him before. No doubt he noticed Coca Mavrodin and me roaming those soggy paths, and, even from a distance, he surely recognized me.

"How the hell did your papers wind up in Colonel Borcan's pocket?"

"It's a bit embarrassing, but he figured I owed him something, so he kept my papers as collateral. Supposedly I owed him a fish that had been sent to him by god-knows-who."

"It's not good to be in debt to a colonel."

Skirting well around the wet meadows to the south, we finally reached the edge of the boggy ground that stretched its bumpy way all the way to Severin Spiridon's fence. By then, though, there was not a sign of life around the farmhouse, neither of the dappled dog nor his master. Coca Mavrodin went over squelching clumps of grass, straight toward the farm.

"Come on, let's take a detour. I'd like to have a word with that man with the binoculars."

But by then, of course, Severin Spiridon was nowhere to be seen. On arriving we found only his boots, placed neatly beside each other in the doorway. Barefoot tracks led through the mud toward the barn. The whining dog could be heard from behind the kitchen door.

"He's hiding," observed Coca Mavrodin. Proceeding to walk through the yard, well ahead of me, she added, "So we'll just have to find him."

There was no lock on the barn door, so Coca Mavrodin opened it. She disappeared into the darkness inside for thirty seconds at most, and by the time I got there she was back out, standing on the threshold. She didn't even bat a dry, leathery eye.

"Got a knife?"

I promptly handed her my mushrooming knife, which I always had on me. She refused.

"I can't reach up there; you do it. Cut him down nice and easy."

Inside the barn, light from gaps in the ceiling—gaps formed by cracks in the roof's ice-smashed tiles—shone through the darkness like glinting blades. There swayed the silhouette of Severin Spiridon, hanging from a rope, the binoculars still around his neck. He was barefoot, but the scent of rubber boots lingered above his limp feet.

Izolda Mavrodin urged me on.

"Hurry up. Before someone thinks I did this."

I went into the barn, perched on the edge of the manger,

and cut him down, like that. Severin Spiridon plopped onto the hay-covered floor. Through the thin rays of light I could see steam still coming from his mouth. Kneeling down beside him, I pinched his cheeks and pressed my lips to his. I puffed and inhaled again and again, giving it my all, until I felt him cough gently into my face. Once his eyelids started quivering, I fetched a pail of water, poured some over his face and neck, and left it there for him to find at hand.

All the while, Coca Mavrodin had been pacing back and forth out front.

"I asked you to cut him down. Not to go kissing him. How on earth did such a thing cross your mind?"

"I only gave it a try—"

"But you revived him."

Severin Spiridon's dog was barking from behind the farmhouse door. Passing by the boots its master had removed, we veered back out to the trail and crossed the meadow to the solitary jeep. Brilliantly colored autumn bugs now covered the dead crow in the puddle on the canvas roof. Wispy clouds frizzed under the peaks above Dobrin, and the squealing of geese resounded like the curt sounds of a track watchman's whistle.

"I'm going to have a smoke," I said. "If you're in a hurry, Miss, don't wait around. I'll be fine. I'll get down on my own. I know the shortcuts."

Coca Mavrodin sat behind the wheel, closed the door behind her, and rolled down her window.

"Do people around here often do this sort of thing?"

"They aren't hooked on it just yet."

"All I'll say is, don't you dare touch a dead man again."

"If I can stay here, I promise. If not, I can't be held responsible for my actions."

"Get one thing through your head: a dead man's job is to never move again."

Often I found cigarette butts around the barracks, and I kept them in a little sheet-metal box in my pocket. Having now picked out a particularly fat one, I slipped it into my cigarette holder. The jeep didn't start, so I lit up and kept puffing away while resting my elbows on the hood. From there I saw Severin Spiridon lying prostrate, his elbows on the threshold of the barn. His saliva still clung to my face.

"Odd, isn't it, that he happened to do it just now?" grumbled Coca Mavrodin. "Precisely when we were coming this way. A bit odd, if you ask me."

"Not really. He had to do it sometime."

"Once he recovers, I'm going to interrogate him. I'll ask him what the hell he was watching through those binoculars. Yes, he can give me a nice little explanation."

"He'll say he wasn't watching anything. Or else just us. I know these types."

Having turned the jeep around, Coca Mavrodin killed the engine and let the vehicle roll silently down the winding mountain road.

"Well," she said, "I know these types, too. He's just trying to get on my nerves."

As the vehicle rolled down from the Baba Rotunda Pass over the pothole-pockmarked road, Coca Mavrodin kept turning the wheel with one hand, and with her other hand poking about in her ear. No doubt her ears were popping constantly. So she wasn't lying: this was the first time she'd been on mountain roads. Once we finally stopped down below, she reached over me and opened my door herself.

"The gray ganders, as you people call them, will take you to the border in the morning. Now get going and forget all about this."

"Too bad," I said. "I was hoping you'd change your mind. I could kick myself over that business involving the fish—that's the root of all my problems."

"What kind of 'fishy business' are you talking about?"

"As I mentioned earlier, Colonel Borcan was looking for a fish and he thought I was hiding it from him."

"A *dead* colonel is not a colonel."

I spent the night—my last one in Dobrin City and the Sinistra Zone, it seemed—at Aranka Westin's. She had a wooden tub fit for bathing. I filled it with warm water. Meanwhile I stirred up more than one shot—denatured alcohol, resin, and water—to get in the right frame of mind to tell her the truth: that within hours I'd be leaving for good. We then sipped away at those spirits, and by resting our feet on each other's shoulders, we managed to squeeze into the tub.

In the middle of the night the gray ganders found me at Aranka Westin's. Still a bit drunk, I lurched out to the jeep in underpants whose moist love splotches froze solid the moment I stepped outside. Coca Mavrodin-Mahmudia's face shone through the brambly darkness like one of those faraway salt-white hills she'd spoken of. With the Sinistra River roaring in the background, she informed me with a shout that she'd had second thoughts: for a while, as long as she saw fit, I could stay on in Dobrin.

"The gray ganders will come up with a nice new name for you—or, what the hell, just keep the old one—it isn't your real one, either."

Coca Mavrodin was an enigmatic woman. A capricious soldier. It seemed that all that time she'd been toying with me: in fact, she'd wanted to keep me on. Years later, on visiting Dobrin, I heard that she had met with a cryptic end. Having dozed off in the woods, she was caught unprepared by a freezing rain, and, motionless, like a sleeping moth, she froze into a crystalline mass under the ice. Later the wind tipped over this block of ice, which broke to pieces and melted. Only a pile of rags remained—it smelled of dead bugs and yes, was pinned all over with colonel's stars.

5

MUSTAFA MUKKERMAN'S TRUCK

Back when I lived in Dobrin, where I'd gone on the trail of my adopted son, there was a single photographer in the entire forest district. And even he worked only for the mountain infantry. Not that his job was to immortalize either camouflaged soldiers trudging up mountainsides or red-lipsticked secretaries at headquarters. No, he was out there pursuing the conservation area's Prussian bears—there were some 130 or 140 of them—for official record-keeping purposes.

Photographer Valentin Tomoioaga, himself a colonel, would roam the woods for weeks at a time. Although his good connections probably meant he received a whole host of inoculations, the Tungusic Flu got him, too, in the end. He fell ill at the edge of the woods above Dobrin City, in a cluster of denuded, barkless spruces that could be seen even from the village. Although he was discovered early on—the trim on his mantle kept fluttering about in the wind, which made him especially easy to spot—Valentin Tomoioaga was not admitted to the sick ward at the barracks. To the contrary, stakes were driven into the ground all around him as he lay there, sprawled out, in the throes of fever. Planks were then nailed all over the stakes, attached by beams the dead spruces—all to ensure that he didn't hobble off somewhere and infect anyone else. Ears of corn were stuck through the gaps in the hastily erected plank fence for the photographer to chew on; as for drink, there was dew.

The Tungusic Flu stirred great dread around there, so it invariably seemed best if those stricken by the contagion, even if they happened to be colonels, were never again allowed back into the barracks, the village, or anywhere else, for that matter.

While no successor was named for the ailing Valentin Tomoioaga, the day soon came when the need arose for a substitute photographer. No, not someone to visit the bears or some top secret site in the conservation area. Instead, the search was on for someone with a camera to head up to the Ukrainian border, where a foreign trucker was expected that very day. This meant there was surely something suspicious about the man, who was none other than the meat-trucker Mustafa Mukkerman, though I myself had often seen him at the wheel of his truck—a silvery vehicle daubed all over with various colorfully painted figures—as he rolled by along the main, north-south highway that skirted its way around Dobrin.

Why was I, of all people, summoned to fill in for the photographer, who by now was sick as a dog and staring death in the face? Granted, I was known to be a jack-of-all-trades, but the decision could solely be chalked up to unpredictable, womanly whim. Indeed, it will forever remain a mystery why Colonel Coca Mavrodin chose me when she might have selected any of the numerous sly, secretive mountain infantrymen.

True, no sooner had she succeeded Puiu Borcan as forest commissioner than their differences became apparent. From my perspective, the winds of change fluttered about on tiny slips of paper, private letters of sorts, on which Colonel Coca Mavrodin summoned me repeatedly to headquarters. That's how it happened in this case, too. One morning near the fruit depot I noticed scraps of paper bags rustling on utility poles, tacked to fences, and tied to tree branches hanging over the road. All bore the same, charcoal-scribbled summons: *"Hurry, Andrei, Miss Coca is waiting for you."*

Izolda Mavrodin-Mahmudia—Coca was her nickname—sat in the armchair of the late Colonel Puiu Borcan with two enormous cameras on the desk before her: a Konica and a blunderbuss of a Canon. It was no problem if I didn't know a whole lot about picture-taking, she said, noting that these machines did practically everything themselves. All they needed was a trustworthy, sensitive soul to hold them, to change the film now and again, and to press the buttons.

The Ukrainian border, where Mustafa Mukkerman was to arrive, ran along the nearby crest of Pop Ivan Mountain. Even from Dobrin, flares could sometimes be seen at night shooting through the air, as could the watchtowers' spotlights as they panned, flashing against the clouds. By day, though, the very same apathy came sliding down the slopes of Pop Ivan Mountain toward the valley as from any nearby peak; nothing much had happened there in decades.

Huddled before me in the commander's chair, Coca Mavrodin was already dressed for the drafty pass, bundled up in a hooded gray greatcoat of the sort worn by the mountain infantry. To protect herself from the wind she'd stuffed her ears with yellow cotton; the sour-bitter stink of bugs hovered about her. Word had it that she'd wound up here in the frigid north from the miasmic delta down south, from that danger-fraught world of giant catfish and pelicans.

"Whenever I have the chance," she said, "I'm pleased to work with civilians. So I thought of you, Andrei. But there will be two more individuals with us, from the younger generation."

It was an amphibious Red Cross military vehicle that took us over streambeds, bogs, and soggy meadows all the way to the foot of Pop Ivan Mountain, then up along a dirt road full of hairpin turns that wound its way to the narrow pass. Behind the wheel was Coca Mavrodin. I sat beside her, cameras hanging heavily from my neck; on the back seat were the gray ganders, two nearly identical young men wearing glum expressions, winter coats, scarves, suits, and oxfords. They were accompanied by a pair of Dobermans that also looked exactly alike.

From our confidential conversation along the way, it turned out that the international trucker Mustafa Mukkerman was arriving from far away with a load of frozen mutton. Passing through once a week on his way to the southernmost reaches of the Balkans, he crossed the border without fail every Thursday at noon.

He was no run-of-the-mill creature. A giant of classic proportions, Mustafa Mukkerman was said to weigh more than half a ton. In the back seat, the two gray ganders were now racking their brains over his colossal limbs, and who would get which side of him once it came time to commence the body search; they'd come along with the aim of finding something on him.

As we made our way up to the border in that amphibious vehicle, at bends in the road we sometimes caught glimpses of Pop Ivan Mountain's weasel-hued bluffs and its rocky crags, pale-red veins which ran down from the summit deep into the forest below. But all this faded as the pass neared and the weather turned worse. Winter arrived with a vengeance that day up there on the heights of Pop Ivan Mountain.

The border station comprised nothing more than a one-room guard booth and a camp tent; the road in front was closed off by a blue-and-yellow iron crossing-bar. This was the highest point along the old dirt road that crossed the mountains, and here the double-sided slopes contracted into what could just about be called a pass. It was a miserable, drafty place of murmuring bluffs and hoary strips of lichen swaying from the spruces and firs. On the distant, translucent horizon glimmered the disquieting colors of the north.

But on this day, by the time we reached the top the weather had taken a sharp turn for the worse. At first this meant a grayish mix of slush and freezing rain splotching incessantly on the vehicle's galvanized iron shell and its plexiglass windshield. Then, suddenly, silence, followed by an increasingly thick veil of feather-sized snowflakes. There we were, deep in the pass, swamped by a wintertime murkiness broken only by the red stars glowing on the border guards' caps.

All at once came a boom of thunder. And although flashes of lightning now repeatedly tore apart the thick veils of snow, one of the guards hung a hurricane lamp on the crossing gate all the same, presumably so its red light might just keep Mustafa Mukkermann from plowing into the bar were he to arrive at the height of the storm. They knew he wouldn't be late: for years now he'd crossed the border every Thursday at noon. He was the punctual type. It was said that on his father's side—the Mukkerman side, that is—Mustafa was partly German.

The Dobermans now lolled about underneath the amphibious vehicle but Coca Mavrodin walked slowly forward to the crossing-bar. The snow kept falling, yet all the while she waited there, resting her elbow on the blue-and-yellow iron bar; so that not even by chance should she miss the moment when Mustafa Mukkerman's headlights would glimmer through the thick white mass of falling snow along the hairpin turns below, on the far side of the pass. Only the puffs of steam occasionally rising up signaled that a living being was bundled in that woolfelt greatcoat there in the biting wind. Before long, just as much snow had piled up on top of her as on the crossing gate and on the nearby open crate of sand kept in case of fire. Above her fur cap a little eddy of snow swirled in the wind, and finally a bird landed on her shoulder.

The dogs were the first to sniff out Mustafa Mukkermann's arrival. The snow-packed gusts of wind had yet to even carry the slightest drone of that still-distant motor bellowing under the weight of all that cargo when the Dobermans began to yawn, in a clear signal that something had caught their attention. The truck, veiled by fleeting clouds of fog, was already ascending the nearest gradient with its full load of frozen mutton. The two dogs, their ears perked and their stubby tails flinching, came out from underneath the vehicle, smudged with oil. Coca Mavrodin, who knew her dogs, and knew just what to make of the fur billowing on their necks, straightened up at once. The snow coating her back cracked, falling to the ground in big soft cakes.

The bird on her shoulder teetered before plopping stiffly with ice-covered wings into the snow. Apparently it had landed on her in order to die. The bird that carries the Tungusic Flu from the north, so it is said, also succumbs to it in the end.

All fell silent on Mustafa Mukkerman's arrival. The wind died down, the snowflakes froze in the air. Only the thick grayness remained, strafed no longer by lightning but by the truck's headlights. The soldiers raised the crossing-bar to let him pass. The silver-painted walls of the truck were daubed with all manner of drivel which could occur only to a trucker who roved homelessly over international borders: an eyesore of blue palm trees and green monkeys against a purple sky on one wall; another wall decorated with a woman's breast, solitary and profoundly drooping.

The two gray ganders now emerged from within the amphibious vehicle and kicked the snow off the truck's license plate to verify that, indeed, this was their man. Touching their fingers to its silver walls they walked around the truck. Shadows of disapproval crossed their eyes at the sight of the cheaply painted figures all over it.

Meanwhile, Mustafa Mukkerman rolled down his window. Stretching out his enormous, bag-like, bare, rounded arm, he made a fist, which he shook a few times by way of greeting—both by bending his elbow and his wrist. The gray ganders looked at each other: were they really seeing this? Hardly a good omen, that much was certain.

Coca Mavrodin elbowed me, as if urging me to get on with it: I could now begin snapping away. When a light flashed under my fingers, she explained, I would have to insert a new roll of film. I peeped through the viewfinder: the decoratively daubed truck, its driver, the two gray ganders, and the two Dobermans came to life at once in miniature on the nonreflecting glass.

In the meantime, Mustafa Mukkerman brought a piece of machinery into operation that opened the wall of the cab and lifted the driver—that colossal sack of skin—out along with his seat before finally lowering him to the ground, where he then got to his feet. Huge, round masses of flesh and blubbery wattles of skin quivered under his red coveralls. The air around him quivered, too, and the snow began to melt. On noticing two gaunt customs officers step from the booth, he waved to them convivially; they must have been old buddies. Then, clutching the grips built onto the side of the truck, no doubt for this very purpose, and jingling his keys, he made his way toward the back to open the cargo-hold, and so allow them to pass their flashlights over the rimy, looming meat. He was about to break the lead seals off the lock when Coca Mavrodin intervened, announcing that they shouldn't waste their time with "this sort of thing."

At which the gray ganders hurried over to Mustafa Mukkerman, stood on either side and commanded him to undress, there and then. This was the colonel's order, they explained, but being a woman, she was reluctant to pronounce it herself, lest he misunderstand her intentions.

"This is my first such job," Colonel Coca Mavrodin quietly observed beside me. "You know, I was posted before on a pelican farm in the tepid south."

"Good luck with it."

The snow was dying down. The gray ganders consoled Mustafa Mukkerman by noting it wouldn't be any warmer in the guard booth—not that he would fit inside anyway. And again they ordered him to strip, the sooner the better.

"Naturally," said the trucker with a nod. "My pleasure."

"Where did you learn our language so well?" Coca Mavrodin called over.

"Where? Oh, just in passing through. Comes through the window, you know."

"You know, I think it's really too bad that things have come to this. And with you of all people, such a respectable man."

"For me it's a pleasant surprise," said the trucker Mustafa Mukkerman with a grin. "I wanted to show you all my dick, anyway."

Coca Mavrodin first looked away, then glanced suddenly at me to gauge from my expression whether she'd heard him right. Pulling a sharpened indelible pencil from her pocket, she seemed intent on writing on her palm, or in the air, what she had just heard, while the two gray ganders stretched out their necks at the fleeting words. As if waiting precisely for this moment, Mustafa Mukkerman now pulled the zipper down over his chest and belly to slip off his clothes. The unusual coveralls seemed custom-tailored to his proportions: hardly had he given the now-unzipped outfit—already slackened here and there—a shake than it fell right off him. All at once, just as a moment before had been requested, he stood there completely naked, his vast folds of flesh quivering amid all those silvery snowflakes.

"Don't think I'm getting a kick out of this," said Coca Mavrodin, turning toward me. "This is not my thing; I can't stand the sight of naked people. But I got a tip-off from our Polish comrades that this individual is planning to smuggle something through our country hidden among his folds of skin. Just what, unfortunately, they didn't say."

Quivering flesh and wattles of fat hung from Mustafa Mukkerman's shoulders, shoulder-blades, and waist like drooping wings; not that such reaches of his body could be recognized as shoulder-blades or a waist. The gray ganders had to grab the two Dobermans by their collars and pull them near, goading them to sniff over the trucker. The dogs couldn't have cared less—Mustafa Mukkerman didn't interest them one bit.

"It would be best," Colonel Coca Mavrodin said after a little while, "if you just handed it over—then we'd be over the hard part."

"I'm not in a rush."

"But I doubt you want my men to put their hands all over you."

"Why not. I love it when someone scratches my dick."

Coca Mavrodin only stood there, the pencil trembling between her fingers as the gray ganders commenced the body search. They probed frills and folds, slowly pulling their fingers hopefully, with feeling, along each trench between those sausages of skin. They even stretched apart Mustafa Mukkerman's ass cheeks, peering somberly inside. And they rocked his scrotum and its sleepy dumplings back and forth. When they completed their job, they hardly dared to look at each other: not even in the most secret pouches and intimate orifices of skin on this Turkish trucker had they found a thing.

Mustafa Mukkerman still stood there with his legs spread wide in a sort of expectant straddle, as if sorry the whole thing was over so soon. From beneath fatty eyelids he glanced about, absentmindedly lifting his feet again and again from the newly formed slush.

"You think there's something to smirk about?" Coca Mavrodin demanded, casting me a sudden stare: "What the hell?"

"First of all," replied Mustafa Mukkerman in my place, having overheard the question, "I prefer to look respectable in pictures. That aside, I had a dream about this whole thing, and so unfortunately I don't have on me what you were looking for just now."

Coca Mavrodin stared at the gray ganders, and accorded even me another fleeting glance. Then she took that indelible pencil of hers—which no doubt she'd been saving for something or other—and broke it in two at one crack, its halves plopping into the snow. That done, as if signaling that for her the mission was complete, she started off toward the amphibious vehicle with the two stern-faced gray ganders in her wake, and I was turning to follow as well, the cameras heavy around my neck.

Which is when our eyes met—mine and Mustafa Mukkerman's. His were full of goodness, affection, velvety human warmth. Extending a hand toward me, he curled his giant index finger invitingly. From his glove compartment he then fished out a pack of Kents; a little cellophane bag of Haribo fruit gummies; and finally, from somewhere or other, he produced a Kinder chocolate egg, the hollow sort with a toy hidden inside. He offered all this to me on his enormous outstretched palm. Yes, on that sleety morning there in the mountain pass, on the very day that winter arrived, a stark naked Turk gave me—the recently sacked wild berry expert—gifts.

"Listen," he whispered: "No doubt one day you'll get tired of all this. Just let me know. I'd be glad to take you with me to the southern Balkans. Down to Thessaloniki, the Dardanelles, Rhodes. I'll stick you in the back with the sheep. You won't be warm, but you'll come dressed for the occasion. No one will find you in there."

"Please stop."

"Get yourself a nice thick sheepskin coat, the sort that reaches down to your heels. I pass by here every Thursday, stopping at the gas station—you know the one, down on the main north-south highway. But you can also flag me down along the road. Just try to make sure it's not raining that Thursday: if there's one thing you can't do, it's sit among those icy hunks of meat, in the freezer, in wet clothes. All right, you'd better go—Allah be with you."

"I have no idea what you're talking about. I haven't heard a thing—but you really do know the language."

"Nonsense. I only parrot words from memory."

The amphibious vehicle was waiting for me, its motor running, its galvanized iron shell trembling. No sooner did I take my seat than Coca Mavrodin headed off, slipping and sliding over the fresh snow, to descend slowly along the serpentine road toward the Sinistra valley. Already sucking on a Haribo gummy, I looked back, between the heads of the two gray ganders at the fading scene out the rear window: Mustafa Mukkerman still standing there naked in the snow, gazing after us until he disappeared behind our first curve.

"I bet he invited you to come along to the Balkans," remarked Coca Mavrodin. "To the coast of Greece, to Olympia."

"He touched on the notion."

"Well, don't get all excited about such plans just now."

After reaching the bottom of the valley and cutting back across the streambed, the vehicle floundered across those soggy meadows once again. Bracing on their forelegs, the two Dobermans gazed out the window and the gray ganders' eyes sparkled with alertness, though there could hardly have been much worth noting down there in the valley. On nearing the village, Coca Mavrodin, her forehead glistening with sweat, asked me to adjust her cap.

"Next time I'll surprise him," she said. "Really, I mean it—I'll let the air out of the tires, or maybe I'll have the tubes turned inside-out. So he'll lose his taste for us forever."

"And," offered one of the gray ganders, "to think he dreamt about it ..."

"I bet our Polish comrades were playing a trick on us," observed the other.

57

"I suggest you two keep your traps shut," said Coca Mavrodin.

Soon, Mustafa Mukkerman whizzed by along the main highway, his truck daubed all over with palm trees, monkeys, and that solitary, drooping woman's breast. Of course he noticed the amphibious vehicle floundering over the meadow, glassy from sleet—he gave a long honk and waved. The snow his truck had whipped up swirled about and sparkled in his wake: he'd brought winter with him, but he was heading for the sunny Balkans.

The wild fruit depot, where I lived at the time, stood outside the village alone on a meadow and could be reached from the Dobrin railway station only by way of a narrow wagon track. Coca Mavrodin braked at the turn and, after I jumped from the still-moving vehicle, cut the engine.

"Of course I won't have the tubes cut out of his tires," she called after me. "Don't believe such things about me. I knew he had nothing on him. "

"I figured you were just kidding about the tires."

"And if you think about it, you'll realize the whole thing was planned this way in advance with our Polish colleagues—it was a drill."

"I guessed as much."

"No, you didn't. You learned this key bit of information only now, from me: I let you in on it."

Winter was descending in those very hours down the slopes of Pop Ivan Mountain into the Sinistra valley. Icicles were forming from the water trickling over the eaves of the former mill that now functioned as the fruit depot. I had the impulse to crack open my chocolate egg—what sort of clever little trifle lay hidden inside? But now with autumn nearly over, darkness came early, so I saved that pleasant moment for the next day. In the pitch-black hallway I dipped my mug haphazardly into the fermented fruit juices with which I flavored my regular drink, watered-down denatured alcohol. Then I crouched in my little nook in the corner of a storage room, where each night, the spirits lit me up inside out by lighting up my veins.

Before long I was hungry, so I soaked mushrooms and cold boiled potatoes in the watered-down denatured alcohol, then sucked away at this concoction while blissfully perking my ears to the organ-like tunes outside: the wind playing against icicles. In keeping with my habit—rain or shine, every night—I knelt down by the window before dozing off and pissed into the yard.

But, now, my timing wasn't so good. No sooner had I laid down than a beam of light started bouncing its way amid the barrels on those moldy floors and about the dank walls until finally zeroing in on my straw mattress in the corner. And who stood there but one of the gray ganders, sopping wet.

"Please don't do that again," he said softly, sternly. "If you've got to take a piss, we'll be happy to walk you across the dark yard any time. From now on you'll always find one of us nearby."

Of course, I should have guessed as much: from this day on I ranked among Coca Mavrodin's confidants. I'd glimpsed one of her secrets, so from now on the gray ganders would keep an eye on me, too. In proof of which one of them already stood there before me, slushy with piss.

Around dawn, when, in keeping with propriety, I got up to trudge to the outhouse at the far end of the yard, I said to him:

"You've got to be tired. If you come inside, I'll dig up some sacks you can lay down on. A new day's about to begin, get some rest."

"No way," he said, brushing me off. "You're a stranger. How do I know what sort of bed you're offering me?"

"Then forget I said anything."

Morning was at hand. No sooner did the sunlight pour over the slopes than the barking of dogs billowed up; then, along the road, beyond the stream, the mist around the bust of Géza Kökény began glowing yellow.

The barking came again and again. Whenever it ceased for brief intervals, the dead silence would be broken by a howl from Valentin Tomoioaga—the photographer-cum-colonel whose shoes I'd filled for all of a day, and whom I had to thank for Mustafa Mukkerman becoming my friend.

6

ELVIRA SPIRIDON'S HUSBAND

It's said that meeting up with a dwarf in the morning is a good omen. And indeed, early in the day on one of the luckiest days of my life—when Elvira Spiridon and her velvety behind moved in with me—I'd crossed paths with Gábriel Dunka, the dwarf. In Dobrin City, back when both of us were just scraping by, he was among the few people authorized to keep a pair of scissors at home, and I would go over for a trim occassionaly. The one actual barber, Aranka Westin's live-in lover, had been kicked out of town, so when the hair grew out over the nape of my neck, I went to the dwarf for a cut.

On that memorable day—I must have thought it was a Thursday—I had been keeping a lookout for Mustafa Mukkerman, the Turkish trucker, who on that day of the week invariably passed along the north-south highway outside the village. I met up with Gábriel Dunka only by chance. Though autumn was nearly over, and the edges of the stream were already rimmed with ice, I found him sitting on the bank, soaking his wounded, purple-blue ankles in the frigid water. He worked with sand; which is to say, he stomped his feet all day long in a crate full of wet sand in the little workshop where he also lived; the repetitive work chafed his ankles. The Sinistra prison, then under construction, had commissioned him to frost sheets of glass destined for the prison windows. Being the Zone's only dwarf, he alone was suited for the delicate task: the glass didn't break under his light, bantam frame. Even in the dead of winter Gábriel Dunka loped down to the stream, to holes in the ice, to relieve his swollen ankles.

And there he was, swashing his feet about in the stream when I happened upon him. I hadn't planned to chat with him for long, but I stayed there for quite a while. I asked whether he'd seen Mustafa Mukkerman parked at the gas station with his meat truck, or if maybe he had already passed by. But neither of us was quite sure it was in fact Thursday. Indeed, some presentiment to the contrary must have come over me, for I decided then and there to have my hair trimmed a bit—and not just the usual haircut such as I'd gotten not long before, for Colonel Puiu Borcan's funeral.

Snipping away with the scissors behind my ears like a real barber, Gábriel Dunka regaled me with stories. Soon he'd be rich, he announced: some people from the Zone's natural history collection had been around his place lately expressing interest in his skeleton. They said they'd buy it for good money to put on exhibit someday. In his initial anger he'd sent them packing, but if they were to return—and of course such hucksters could hardly be expected to give up so easily—he wouldn't turn them down. Not being particularly interested in his affairs, I asked Gábriel Dunka to keep his mind on the glinting scissors instead, as if even then I knew that I was making myself pretty for none other than Elvira Spiridon.

But just at that moment, as I was getting my haircut in Gábriel Dunka's glass workshop, the mountain infantrymen tracked me down. Without delay they took me to the barracks. Waiting for me in the forest commissioner's office was Coca Mavrodin: she asked me to leave the village that very day and move to the Baba

Rotunda Pass. Under a topographic map of the conservation area, huddled inertly in her greatcoat like a spider in a far corner of its web, she seemed not to have stirred for hours: her eyes, lips, and tongue gave off not even the smallest sparkle of light.

"A road worker lived in the pass," she began, "named Zoltán Marmorstein or something like that. Who in the hell knows what came over him—he up and left—left, just like that. His cabin is empty and I'd like you to move in."

"I wouldn't want to shove him out of his place."

"Look, this individual won't return. If you believe what people say, he made a big scene last night—he cut out his own guts."

"Well, in that case, how could I say no?"

"The road worker's cabin is an official residence, so you will be required to perform certain duties. Zoltán Marmorstein worked for us as a coroner's assistant on the side."

"I'm honored of course that you thought of me. But there's a thing or two I still got to learn about this line of work."

"Good, start learning."

Though she herself had only gone there for the first time in my company, Colonel Coca Mavrodin now suddenly turned around and pointed to the wall map. Tracing a finger along the road that twists and turns its way up to the Baba Rotunda Pass, she pointed out the coal-burning lots scattered over the clearings, and finally, up top, the cabin of the road worker Zoltán Marmorstein. Every single sheep pen, shed, and doghouse had been drawn onto the map, as well as the trails which lay like netting over the pass. I knew the area well.

"And what will I be doing up there?"

"Nothing. You'll just live there—and not alone."

At this, the colonel pulled a bundle of photos from a drawer and spread them over her desk. They depicted local women, most of whom I knew from the fruit depot, where they'd shown up one after another with baskets on their backs full of blueberries, blackberries, and bolete mushrooms. I knew all the harvesters.

"Go ahead—choose," said Coca Mavrodin, pointing at the scattered photos, and then pushing them by turns before me. "Just one for now, naturally."

Among them was that lovely waxwing, Elvira Spiridon. The tip of her nose, her rounded forehead, and her two big brass earrings sparkling even in a photo. The very woman from the sole of whose foot I'd once removed a thorn.

"Choose, and rest assured that any one of them will be happy to move in with you." The colonel momentarily covered the photo of Elvira Spiridon. "Yes, even her."

"Miss Coca," I said, shaking my head in embarrassment, "you're too kind. I hardly deserve this. And then, of course, there are other considerations."

"Don't worry. I've already spoken with her husband. He'll let her go."

Although I knew my way around the Baba Rotunda Pass— and the wall map in the forest commissioner's office had also helped me get oriented—a soldier drove me to the top in a jeep for a brief survey.

The old dirt road—which the Sinistra bus jolted over on its route once a day, carrying mostly bear keepers and mountain infantrymen—followed the drafty watershed up to the top and then back down into the Bukovina hills. On this day the wind, having picked up its pace with the passing of the silent days of autumn, kept whipping clouds across the mountain meadows. At the highest point stood the road worker's cabin. Covered by water droplets, the house had a protruding, glass-enclosed verandah: from the porch, when the clouds broke, this or that hairpin turn in the road below sparkled of tar. Socks left behind by Zoltán Marmorstein hung on a clothesline tied to one of its crack-filled walls.

Besides what fit in my pockets, back then I owned a tin plate, two sheet-metal mugs, a horse blanket, a couple of socks, a few odd shreds of fabric, some cord, and a bottle of denatured alcohol. I returned to the old water mill and I stuffed all this into a satchel. Flinging it over my shoulder, and waved good-bye to the fruit depot, to all those barrels with their intoxicating aromas. Then I headed off to my new workplace, the morgue, which stood in a dank corner of the barracks.

Still anxious to know what had become of Mustafa Mukkerman—and, in particular, to learn how much taking two people to the southern end of the Balkans amid those rimy hunks of frozen meat would cost—I stopped off along the way at Gábriel Dunka's place. He told me, however, that I'd be waiting for the Turk in vain that day: Géza Kökény had been by to see him, and in the course of conversation it turned out that it wasn't Thursday but, at most, Wednesday.

So my first day of work in the Dobrin morgue probably fell on a Wednesday.

It is the duty of a coroner's assistant to sit in a room with the deceased and keep watch, making sure that the subject does not stir during his shift. There, on the dank concrete table, lay the former road worker, Zoltán Marmorstein, his trousers full of guts. He did not stir. Those drying socks of his were indeed now mine.

Evening came and Colonel Titus Tomoioaga arrived for his shift. Out in the fresh air, taking frequent gulps from my bottle while trudging my way up to the Baba Rotunda Pass, I was filled with an inexplicable delight. Snowflakes were melting on my face and as the flurries began the moon shone through the hurtling clouds.

By the time I reached the top, snow was gusting on all sides of the road worker's cabin. Just as I was about to swing the flashlight beam over the steps, I noticed that the verandah window was all steamed up: a scarlet fog flickered and flashed repeatedly from the blazing fire light. So Coca Mavrodin had not been kidding. I was no longer alone.

Inside, the three little red windows of the stove door shone brightly, and a pair of brass earrings sparkled amid the flittering light. Elvira Spiridon sat on the edge of the cot, hands in her lap. Before her were her sandals, removed.

"From now on, sir, I'm living with you."

"Welcome."

"They said you're a man of few words—so perhaps I'll just keep quiet, too."

"Well, let's hope you won't have any reason to complain."

Two thoroughly stuffed round pillows now lay on Zoltán Marmorstein's abandoned cot, along with two freshly washed rag-knit throw rugs—rugs that still smelled of the north wind that had arrived sweeping the pass that day. On the table: an old black cooking pot containing potato soup with a mousy bouquet, half of which had, it seemed, been eaten by someone else. Also on the table, the mountain infantry's favorite drink: a full bottle of blackberry brandy. Pinned atop its cork, a glittering star of sorts: a silvery golden thistle petal.

"It's from my husband."

"Your husband's very kind. I'm sure I'll get to know him too. But for now all I'd ask—if you please—is that you don't start crying."

"My husband is Severin Spiridon—you already know him, sort of."

"The name doesn't ring a bell."

"Well, he got himself into a stupid little mess, and then you came along and helped him. He was ready to give up, but you, sir, came along and breathed life back into him."

"Ah, that's right—I remember—and don't you two have a lovely dappled dog as well?"

"Yes—and our dog hasn't forgotten you either, sir"

Noticing the sock stir around her ankles, I knelt down before Elvira Spiridon and unwound it —from that delicately veined, hay-scented, warm foot, which I'd already had the good fortune to get to know, in a manner of speaking, what with that certain matter involving a thorn. Now I held that foot once again in my palm.

"Ah," I mumbled, momentarily distracted, "colonels keep their word, one way or other. And yes, I thought Coca Mavrodin was just pulling my leg. Bless her a thousand times."

"Yes, it's the colonel's wish that I live with you from now on, sir. But if you'll let me, I'd like to go home now and then."

"Go whenever you please—you have someone to go home to—just now, please, don't start crying."

Uncorking the bottle, I poured some of Severin Spiridon's gift into two sheet-metal mugs. I found a metal washbasin under the cot, which I filled with water and placed on the stove. Then I tried the potato soup. Hot water started bubbling in all directions, and soon the washbasin overflowed, but meanwhile I'd tasted the brandy: I waved a hand toward Elvira Spiridon to signal that it was time to go ahead, get undressed.

I heard that very singular swishing of clothes mixed with the sound of naked arms and velvety thighs nestling against each another and allowed a long time to pass—with those sounds of water trickling over ribs, and even the sound of skin drying.

But then I chose a vein on Elvira Spiridon's thigh that, on its ascent, branched out before coming together again. With an index finger I began following its course upward with apparent hesitation.

"You should know," I said softly, surprised at my own voice, "that I once found a thorn in your foot. I pulled it out with my own teeth."

"I haven't forgotten you, sir."

"Ever since thinking of you, every time you've come to mind, I've called you something different—a mountain ash berry—a bird—a waxwing."

"I don't exactly understand, sir, but I think you're saying lovely words to me."

"Yes, and to follow up on what I was saying: I'm going to kiss every last inch of you. Just so you know—so there won't be any surprises."

"Just kiss me all over, sir, wherever you want."

Much later, well past midnight, as I was squatting naked in front of the stove trying to get the fire going again, I started musing on my own affairs. Mustafa Mukkerman came to mind as did, of course, Béla Bundasian, my adopted son, whom I hadn't seen in four or five years, although he lived nearby, in the off-limits conservation area. Sooner or later, I hoped, I would find him, and perhaps we could leave together for the sunny Balkans. This woman hadn't moved in with me at the most opportune time, but here she was, panting away beside me. Kneeling, I turned toward the bed and reached under the blanket.

"Was that good, I hope?"

"It wasn't bad, sir."

"Maybe all this was meant to happen, but one fine day I may get up and leave this place behind. I'll tell you a secret: I've got another life."

"I thought so. Did you know Zoltán Marmorstein, sir? He left, too."

"No, I never had the pleasure."

"Maybe he'll return: these are his socks."

"If he comes, he comes. We'll welcome him with open arms."

The blizzard had stopped, and the moonlit peaks shone into the house. In the dead silence the snow began crackling around the house as if Zoltán Marmorstein were approaching with those guts of his weighing down his trousers. Elvira Spiridon slipped out from under the blanket and stepped to the window. For a long time, maybe hours, she just stood there: not unlike those nearby peaks, her shoulders were soft, pink, round. Slipping back in beside me at daybreak, her thighs and her behind were like ice, like glass.

I blew my warm breath everywhere over those frigid limbs, running my nose all along her.

"I haven't even mentioned your smell yet. This spot here, for example, right here on your neck, I like it a lot. I don't think I've smelled that on anyone."

"My husband washed me before I left—he spread hazelnut oil all over me."

"Hazelnuts? I've never heard of such a thing. I definitely want to get to know your husband."

"But you do know him. You once saved his life."

It had been years since I'd rested naked on a rag rug by a hot stove, and now I was breathing in the titillating scent of hazelnuts. What more could I have wanted? It seemed I'd achieved all I could hope for. Yes, here I was indeed, lolling about with Elvira Spiridon's velvety behind in my lap. I'd reached the top . . ."

All at once said Elvira Spiridon said, "I don't know your name yet, sir," rousing me from my reverie.

"That's true, but I promise that I'll tell you soon enough, maybe no later than this evening."

"Because, then, perhaps I'd sometimes call you by your name."

"Yes—all I ask is for a bit of patience—that time will soon come. Maybe you won't believe me, but not long ago I lost my papers, and I urgently need to speak with Colonel Coca Mavrodin about my name. Just now, unfortunately, I cannot say."

"I only thought that if I could call you by name, I'd get used to you sooner, sir."

As she sat up beside me on the cot so early that morning, I'd sometimes for fun look out the window from under her armpit or just above her shoulder. A purple mist veiled the valleys, above which only the tops of the spruces were visible: occasionally crows rose up en masse from out of the mist and flew off toward the cliffs of Pop Ivan Mountain. After a while the rising sun poured light over the snowy peaks.

While the cabin aired itself out, we stood before the open window side by side. Our hands touched, slowly pressing against each other until finally they clasped in reconciliation. Cupped between them there no doubt secretly lurked the name of the person whose footprints wound about the cabin walls like bonds of devotion in the snow.

In the clearing opposite the house warm piles of manure sparkled black in the freshly fallen snow A dappled dog sauntered about between them and waxwings fluttered above, warming themselves in the swirling steam. Smoke hovered in a tangled web above the shingles of the nearby farmhouse: at home, after his nocturnal excursion, Severin Spiridon was already puttering about.

The sun was blazing strong. Soon I had to be off to my new workplace. Plainly there was a woman in the house—I found my fatigue jacket hanging on the fence, awash with fresh air; my first thought was that although I was looking upon official, assistant coroner's garb that there's not a stubborn odor the wind of the pass can't blow right out of such old clothes in a single night.

7

BEBE TESCOVINA'S BLOOD

Early one morning a mountain infantryman dropped in on the assistant coroner— the onetime blackberry and blueberry authority, Andrei—in the road worker's cabin in the Baba Rotunda Pass. The soldier waited until Elvira Spiridon had left, disappearing into the spruces in the direction of her husband's farm, and then he'd stepped from the woods and headed for the cabin, alone there atop the pass. For his part, Andrei Bodor, as soon as he heard the approaching steps—crackling hard on the film of ice coating the road: the sound of someone bringing terrible news—cowered behind the door and, like a dog, pissed a few drops into the corner.

But the soldier brought only a package, one that carried an intimate message. From the satchel that hung at his side he pulled a second-hand uniform—a noncommissioned officer's—along with a pair of rubber boots and tight knee-breeches. He told Andrei Bodor that they were heading off to Dobrin City and to put them on at once.

Andrei knew this couldn't mean anything all that bad. In the Sinistra Zone, such cast-off, chevronless uniforms were worn by the mountain infantry's inside men.

"I came on foot so we'd have time for a chat along the way."

"What's the use of chatting with me? About strawberries, blackberries, and long-eared owls?"

"Then let's just get to the point. If you'll allow me—"

"Why? We don't have much common ground."

"Oh but we do—let's not neglect Miss Coca. She's the one who sent me. At first she misjudged you, but her opinion's changed since then—just between us, she now holds you in high regard. And what's more, she's offering you a very sensitive job—of course, only if you accept, naturally. She'd like to send you to the conservation area."

"I don't have access. Colonel Borcan never gave me permission."

"Well, you've got it now. Miss Coca wants you to spend a night at the commissary. A little girl lives there, Bebe Tescovina. They say her eyes glow at night like a lynx. Miss Coca wants to find out if it's true, and it wouldn't hurt to get to the bottom of this."

Back in the days of mining on the slopes above Dobrin, a narrow-gauge railway had led down to the loading ramps and slag heaps. Later, when ore production ceased and the bears were moved into the abandoned mine shafts, that railway came in handy to deliver fodder, fruit, trash, and horse carcasses—not to mention live donkeys—to those beasts. The former miners' commissary still stood at the last stop on the route: now bear-keepers and forest rangers went there every night to drink, to play nine-men's morris, dice, and dominoes, and to fry mushrooms and bird eggs on the stove.

Everyone around there knew Bebe Tescovina, the daughter of commissary manager Nikifor Tescovina, by her fiery red hair. Indeed, until the first snowstorm buried the railroad tracks, she would fly down to school in Dobrin City on a handcar, her hair like mountain ash berries blazing its way right past the gray gates and the watchful locals. Now it turned out that her eyes blazed too, and I was being asked to find out why.

"I'm no expert in such matters."

"Don't try kidding me. Also, there's a little package waiting for you at the guard booth at the barracks that you are to take to Géza Hutira."

"Géza Hutira ... Géza Hutira, who's that? I haven't had the pleasure of meeting him."

"He's the meteorologist up in the conservation area. You can't miss him, his hair reaches the ground. Hasn't had it cut in twenty-three years."

Andrei Bodor had waited five years for this day. Countless times he'd imagined the moment he and his adopted son would meet again. But not a muscle in his face moved on hearing the news.

"I know nothing about any of this—maybe I wouldn't even find my way there."

"I'm convinced you would."

"You know, I'm not keen on rambling about the forest in the dead of winter. You can guess what I'm thinking: I might catch something. We haven't gotten inoculations yet this year."

"That's true—Miss Coca stopped them. Said she didn't like the idea of her men getting stuck full of pins. Said she'd come up with something else."

The package waiting for Andrei at the guard booth was just a single aluminum pole. Well, not quite a pole, but a contraption of telescopic Popes extendible to quite some distance, with little holes of various sizes from which orange-red and yellow woolen threads dangled. Its purpose was a mystery. Placing it on his shoulder, Andrei headed off.

Across the road the bust of the heroic bear warden Géza Kökény was soot-black, what with the crows perched all over it. But as Andrei approached they flew off, and suddenly the monument shone snow-white from their droppings. This was both a good omen and not. The Red Cross jeep stood nearby, Coca Mavrodin's moth-dusted face behind its window. One would not have taken her for a woman, had it not been for the pendant around her neck, emitting a fiery glitter: a five-pointed red star encased in a brass frame.

By the end of autumn passing snowfalls had only flecked the lower reaches of forest with gray slush, and even this had quickly melted off from the railway embankment and the narrow-gauge tracks. Andrei, the aluminum pole on his back, trudged right to the station to take the line-inspection handcar out to the conservation area: the tracks ended there, in front of Nikifor Tescovina's commissary.

Halfway there, at the preserve entrance, a crossing gate barred the tracks. In his guard booth Colonel Jean Tomoioaga, noticing from a distance who was approaching, stepped onto the embankment to open the gate for Andrei.

Andrei applied the brakes and tied the handcar to the crossing gate to keep it from rolling back down the incline. The colonel, seeing that Andrei was in no hurry, pulled out the chess set from underneath his cot. Beside an open door they spread out a canvas board on the floor and pushed the ungainly little carved figures about: should anyone appear, the whole thing could be swept up in one motion.

Knowing that his friend had never gone beyond the fence, Colonel Jean Tomoioaga cautioned Andrei that after the crossing gate the grade began to ascend steeply, so it wouldn't hurt to grease the axles thoroughly before heading out. The tallow was in a tub under the eaves of the guard booth, and in the tub was a broad wooden shovel. After the game, while Andrei went about smearing tallow over the axles, the colonel examined the aluminum pole. Extending it, he pulled the Popes out from one another until he noticed the name of the late forest commissioner, Colonel Puiu Borcan, engraved on one of the middle components.

So, even if the late colonel was not to be buried, it seemed then that the spot where he lay nailed to the ground and covered with plastic bags was to be marked with the bright aluminum pole, which could be seen from afar. The colored strings, meanwhile, especially the orange-red ones, would be visible even in thick fog, and the wind would whistle through the holes. Thus the spot could be located even at night if necessary, and even once entombed by blizzards.

"The soldiers who found him," added Colonel Jean Tomoioaga, "say he was already a bit nibbled. By bats, of course."

"Oh yes," grumbled Andrei. "Very funny. Bats hibernate in winter."

Having unfastened the handcar, Andrei stood behind the crank and drove on. Alongside the stream gushed downward with blinding clusters of foam, its din completely obscuring for him the creaking of the handcar. The sound of the wheels resounded far along the tracks, however—all the way to the last station, buzzing and droning in the trestles that signaled the end of the platform. It could be heard even in the commissary: when the handcar appeared around the final curve, Nikifor Tescovina was already waiting with folded arms at the end of the track.

"You're looking for my little girl," he said by way of greeting. "Unfortunately she's not here. She went for a walk with Géza Hutira."

Though winter was descending down the mountainsides in banks of roving gray mist, Nikifor Tescovina stood about in the mud with an uncovered head, in a tank top and moth-eaten army trousers, his bare feet in leather sandals. The mud around him was full of children's barefoot tracks.

"First I'll go find the meteorologist," said Andrei. "On the way back I'll spend the night here."

"Yes, I know. But I might already be asleep, so let's knock back a shot or two right now."

The commissary comprised a single, dank room that smelled

of mushrooms. At one end was a makeshift bar, behind which was a stove, ringed by sundry kitchen implements and appliances; in the corner, a wide cot. The three bear wardens cowering about in the room wore high-collared fatigue jackets glossy with grime, and cuirassed and otherwise covered with iron fittings and rivets—perhaps as protection against bear scratches. The chief warden, Doc Oleinek, was sprawled alone at a table, while the albino twins sat drinking on a narrow bench by the wall, arm in arm. According to the sheet-metal dog tags hanging from their necks, their names—and even among twins this is extremely rare—were the same: each was called Hamza Petrika. Seeing Andrei for the first time, they kept sticking their tongues out at him.

Nikifor Tescovina's two dark-haired children now appeared as well, lured by the brilliantly-colored aluminum pole. They licked the glistening Popes and ran their fingers over the inscribed letters. They'd been the last to see Colonel Puiu Borcan alive; from the commissary the forest commissioner had headed off toward his final resting place. The colonel had been nearly transparent, so close was he to death: beside the table where he'd sat one last time to drink some hot spiced wine, only his outline trembled; translucent from fever, his great big flaccid ears had sparkled like crumpled cellophane. By the time they found him, so it was said, he'd already been nipped at and then some.

"I'm afraid I'll be disturbing you a bit tonight."

"Go ahead and come. As I say, I know what's up."

The trail that led to the meteorologist's cabin started at the bottom of a narrow dale across a meadow full of tiny mounds from the commissary. At the edge of this meadow was Gábriel Dunka, the dwarf, roaming about among the mounds on all fours. He wore shoulder-length gloves, and from time to time stuck his entire arm into the ground, into a mysterious little shaft. For a long time he'd been doing business on the side with

Nikifor Tescovina, catching marmots for him in the commissary meadow: every time a train or a hand-operated trolley approached on the tracks, the marmots streamed out among the mounds.

"Listen here," Andrei called to the dwarf, "there's no one around just now. I know all about your business—You're crawling with cash. Let me borrow some."

"You've got me cornered. Just how much would you need?"

"I was thinking four twenties. I'll pay you back sooner or later, I swear. I need exactly four bills. My life depends on it."

"Keep going now—Nikifor Tescovina's standing behind the window."

The valley widened a bit halfway to Géza Hutira's cabin, and there a crimson spring trickled out of the ground into a tiny pool that fed into the main stream. It was called the Crooning Spring: the wind crooned night and day amid the mouths of the empty bottles that had been tossed into the adjacent nettle. Carbonated mineral water poured forth from the Crooning Spring, daubing the walls of the pool with rust; a furry crimson film covered the stones, the spruce bark roots, everything the water trickled over. It even smelled of blood.

And in fact it was a bit bloody. Bebe Tescovina stood above the spring splashing herself with water. Having removed her sweat suit, she was lolling about on a rock, wearing nothing but a diaper of sorts even as the frost and rime everywhere in the shade blazed coolly pink. Narrow veins of blood trickled all over her spindly, child's thighs, her bony legs.

Géza Hutira was sitting on a stump. Just now it wouldn't have been possible to recognize him from his ankle-length hair—that was tucked under his clothes at his neck. The aromatic smoke from his Pope, filled with thyme, drifted far. An empty bottle crooned away near his legs. Through drifting veils of smoke he scrutinized the slight body of Bebe Tescovina and the circuitous trails of blood on those scrawny, water-glistening thighs. He noticed Andrei, whose approach was cloaked by the din of the stream, only when the aluminum pole on his shoulder glistened.

"How d'you do?" he greeted Andrei. "I figured someone would come round looking for me today. Let's be off so you can make it back in time." Rising from the rock, the Pope clenched between his teeth, he stretched and called over to Bebe Tescovina. "I've got a little business with this gentleman. If you could manage it, come here tomorrow this time of day."

Only Bebe Tescovina's short red hair shone just now: not for a moment did she remove her eyes—eyes as bloomy and blue as blueberries—from Géza Hutira. As the two men headed off she slowly dressed, plainly disappointed.

The trail kept disappearing into the streambed, and it was apparent that the one man who walked it always wore rubber boots. The edges of the little pools of water along the way up were already covered by a skin of ice, and wagtails were dipping into those pools from their perches on glassy-glazed rocks and glistening branches.

"Live on your own?" asked Andrei, almost gasping for breath from the ascent.

"You mean me? Why do you ask?"

"Just curious how you live. I also love being on my own. Maybe we've got that in common."

"In common, huh?" said Géza Hutira, giving the other man an almost sympathetic once-over. "That all depends. But I'll tell you—there's a fellow that lives with me. You'll meet him, in any case."

Géza Hutira's cabin stood at the far end of the valley, above the tree line, amid boulder piles and the sparkling rivulets that ran between them. There, the thick forest had turned suddenly sparse, with only a few aging, odd old spruces weighed down by graybeard lichen clutching to the slopes, cut here into rifts.

The clouds must have risen from there not long before—the wood-shingle roof was still glistening with rainbows of water droplets. Nearby and likewise gleaming nearby was a white, four-legged hut containing the meteorologist's instruments; a bit further off, motionless crows huddled atop several small observation devices positioned under the open sky.

Sitting on the cabin's doorstep—his hands clenched as if in prayer, but twirling his thumbs, and with an overturned bottle of denatured alcohol by his feet—was Béla Bundasian, Andrei's adopted son. Beset by the early baldness common among Armenians, his tall brown forehead loomed large, and that, together with his bushy eyebrows and the thick lenses underneath, gave him a slightly owlish visage. From behind his glasses he cast his stepfather a rigid glance, bereft of either joy or surprise. He hardly stirred when Andrei, the aluminum pole on his shoulder, stopped in front of him.

"You," he muttered, as if talking only to himself: "How the hell did you get here?"

"I've been looking for you," whispered Andrei. "For five years I've been on your trail."

"On my trail? But why?"

"Yes, I managed to outwit them—I wanted to see you—and now I'm here."

"And you came to see me—that's it?"

"I don't have anyone besides you."

Taking the empty bottle, Béla Bundasian patiently held it upended at his mouth: until finally, a few last drops came out. Then, after a prolonged effort to hawk up some phlegm, he spat and shook his head. "Terrible."

Taking a pair of binoculars, Géza Hutira stepped out of the cabin: he scanned the ridgeline above the cold, deep river basin before finally setting his sights on a barren height shining with freshly fallen snow. As he peered through the lenses, the sharp crest of a pile of rocks trembled before him: Colonel Borcan lay there covered with plastic bags. The aluminum pole was to be planted beside him.

"I see you've come across an old acquaintance," Géza Hutira remarked casually, handing Andrei the binoculars. "But you can count on my discretion. I won't ask any questions."

"Thank you, and yes, I know him—and I'd like a word with him."

"While you two talk things over, I'll cover my ears, or maybe I'll go for a little walk."

"Oh, no need for that," Béla Bundasian interjected. "Don't plug your ears. Why should he think I've got secrets to keep from you?"

Before long the three had climbed up to the plateau, which was covered by a snow dusting that looked like a mix of poppy seeds and powdered sugar. Dusk was coming on, and ice shone from the rifts in the mountainside above them—ice that gave away the winding trails Géza Hutira traversed on his way up to the rock ledges where he read his instruments. And now, having donned crampons and with a steel wire wound around his waist, he set off for the ledges on his own, the aluminum pole on his shoulder.

By the time he reached the saddleback and, eventually, the pile of rocks at the foot of which Colonel Puiu Borcan lay covered, it was already pretty dark. Down below, Andrei waited quietly with his adopted son, watching the distant figure projected against the sky until, finally, from one moment to the next, it vanished in the descending dusk. As night fell, an enormous bat suddenly swooped down over the plateau, its shadow rocking back and forth above the hoarfrost-covered mountain spruces and junipers until it, too, flitted off into the darkness—the late forest commissioner's stray, ownerless umbrella.

All at once the wind stopped dead in its tracks and, as if into an empty bottle, silence fell between the bare walls. From high above, the sound of metallic hammering and tinkling could be heard where Géza Hutira was driving the aluminum pole into the ground, wedging in stakes all around it, the taut wires twanging. The murmur of the streams below rose up in curtains from out of the valley, like fog after a rain.

"I read your diary," Andrei began, "thinking it would tell me what business you'd got mixed up in."

"That was a really, really bad idea."

"That's why I first looked for you over at Connie Illafeld's, though that was in vain. And that's also how I realized that you were in a lot worse trouble than I'd thought."

"I don't know what sort of trouble you're talking about—the trouble is you looking at my diary."

"I had to. I needed to know what might have happened to you."

"You know full well how much I hate that sort of thing—and as you can see, nothing's happened at all."

"All the same I found you in the end. I've been looking for you for years now, and nowadays I live nearby in Dobrin. I'll take you away from here."

"Forget about it—right this instant! Don't bother about me anymore. I'm fine here on my own."

"I'll come get you sometime in the spring or, latest, early summer. Like I said, I've got no one besides you."

"Well, just don't imagine I'll go with you. I'm staying put, and if you don't leave me alone, I'll make it my business to get word out about just what you're after here in the forbidden zone."

It seemed that Géza Hutira had finished his work, that the aluminum pole was now planted firmly among the rocks and tied down tight by taut wires, because all at once the wind stirring its way over the ridgeline began whistling through its boreholes. Soon stones began tumbling down the slopes with his approaching steps. Then the swooshing of his hurricane lamp could be heard, but Géza Hutira knew every contour of the mountainside so well that he lit it only on getting to the bottom, near the two waiting men, and suddenly the entire slope began to glitter: the rocks underneath the thin veil of snow were glowing under the lamplight—blue, green, and copper flickerings spread in waves over the scene.

Long before the bears were brought in, ore had been mined on the slopes of Dobrin and a cableway had once operated, running from the plateau down into the valley to the loading platform of the narrow gauge railway; at the supporting columns, where the mine buckets had jolted over the pulleys, a few nuggets of ore would invariably tumble out. And so it was that now these fallen pieces of ore glistened silkily under the snow.

After the mining operations along the slopes had been closed down, it was the meteorologist Géza Hutira who'd moved into the cabin there, which had been home to the cableway's onetime maintenance man, cobbled together out of rocks and beams. With its mossy rocks and its lichen-draped, fog-drenched beams, the cabin seemed as if it had grown there on its own; it belonged to the mountainside. As the lamplight spread out, the place filled up with scurrying shadows.

"Don't be scared of them," said Géza Hutira. "Weasels and mole rats are man's best friends."

Stretching out on a pile of rags in a corner, Béla Bundasian opened a bottle, flooding the cabin with the scent of yellow gentian roots thoroughly soaked in liquor.

"I'll bring you a blanket," Andrei said in an effort to kick-start a conversation. "It won't be easy, but I'll have one stolen from some warehouse."

"No, I hate blankets."

"I'm sure that next time I'll come by with good news. I've got an acquaintance, a trucker. He's a foreigner.

"What are you talking about? And anyway by now you're one of them, after all. Otherwise you wouldn't be here."

"That was the only way I could get near you."

"Well," said Béla Bundasian "I don't want to see you again." He pulled a tattered coverlet and some assorted rags over his head as he turned toward the wall. "And forget all this crap, I don't talk with foreigners, or with natives, either. And I know full well how to get rid of anyone who wants to get me involved in some screwed-up business."

"Time to get lost," said Géza Hutira, elbowing Andrei in the side. "You're bothering him—I know Béla, he's sensitive. And besides, Nikifor Tescovina is waiting for you back down at the commissary."

Although he had a flashlight, Andrei didn't use it in the thickening darkness lower in the valley: the stream, shimmering under the starlight, unfurled before him like a ribbon of silk and led his way to the commissary. There, Nikifor Tescovina, a hurricane lamp swinging from his hands, awaited his guest.

"I pushed two tables together for you," he said. "The kids spread freshly cut spruce boughs over them. We eat in the morning, so you can already settle in for the night."

The tart scent of denatured alcohol and yellow gentian roots wafted over from the wide plank bed where Nikifor Tescovina and his three children slept. They'd extinguished the lamp, and the fire in the stove had long gone out—the only sound to be heard was their thick gulps as they passed the bottle. Deep within the darkness shone Bebe Tescovina's eyes.

Spiders and larvae hissed inside the walls; dormice, weasels, and bats began stirring in the attic; tiny nails clicked across the floor. Heavy sleeping breaths wove their webs through the entire commissary. When Nikifor Tescovina arose, barefoot, causing the floorboards to creak as he stepped across the room, day was breaking. Andrei, too, sprang up from the tables he'd been sleeping on to stand on the threshold beside the commissary manager. Heads down, they stood there side by side pissing on the steps, staring at the foaming, steaming streamlets, a web of narrow black veins winding their way over the rimy earth. The dark membranes in the valley's nooks and crannies hardly shimmered, but high up on the ridgelines of Dobrin, the aluminum pole glittered like the star of daybreak.

No sooner did daylight come than the children crawled out from under the blankets and Nikifor Tescovina started up the fire. They roasted hazelnuts, shriveled plum, custard mushrooms, and acorns on the hot stove while blueberry tendrils soaked in a pot of water. Fragrant steam coated the cold windows in an instant. To see outside, Bebe Tescovina ran her palms over the glass.

"Is this man going to live here?" she asked.

"I don't know yet," replied her father.

"He could have my place if he needs it, I'll move away. Géza Hutira promised to take me in. Maybe even today I'll get out of here forever."

"Go ahead, if that's what you want. I'll let you go."

After breakfast, Andrei said goodbye to Nikifor Tescovina, but as he walked across the narrow, rime-frosted meadow toward the train tracks, Nikifor sidled up beside him.

"What do you think," asked Nikifor Tescovina, "about that fellow living up there at Géza Hutira's?"

"Nothing much."

"But that wasn't the first time you've seen him?"

"Well, you could say that."

"Just so you know: last night he went to the village. He's not supposed to, and in fact he never does."

Andrei was leaning over the bumper at the end of the tracks and unfastening the chain of the handcar, when he slowly stood up straight, patted his belly, opened his mouth wide, and threw up on the handcar's seat. Bits of wild mushrooms quivered under knots of coagulated blood in the thick, sparkling slime.

"You've got an upset stomach."

"No, no—it's just that I leaned over and it tumbled out of me."

"Good god, looks like your gray matter."

Andrei wiped off the seat with his palm, sat down, and released the brake using the hand crank, so the handcar would head off down the slope on its own.

"Not even I understand," said Nikifor Tescovina, "why the kid's eyes light up in the dark. But it only started recently, after her first period."

"Well then, that's what I'll tell them."

"Then they should also know that she's planning to move away. It's best if the higher ups have plenty of time to digest any change."

"Yes, all right, I heard so, too, and I'll report it just that way."

"Of course, don't keep quiet about the fact that it's Géza Hutira who's taking her in."

"Okay," said Andei Bodor, "rest assured I'll report exactly that."

8

HAMZA PETRIKA'S LOVE

The two Hamza Petrikas worked on Doc Oleinek's bear reserve in the Dobrin conservation area and impaled themselves on one of the last nights of autumn. A couple of days before, they'd been seen in the village: it was Revolution Day, and the game wardens had a holiday. They had been loitering about all afternoon in front of the knife-throwers' tent, which was pitched on the bank of the Sinistra alongside those of the other showmen. Now, the Hamza Petrikas may have had their eyes trained on those glinting blades as they hit their target one after another, but the people standing were staring at them instead. No one had ever before seen two young men—blue skin, red eyes, feather grass hair—who looked so much alike. Albino twins, they so resembled each other that even their thick, bearwarden overalls creased at the very same places; and, judging by the way that steam issued from their nostrils simultaneously, they even breathed in sync. But to top it all off: the little sheet-metal dog tag hanging from their necks proclaimed that they both were called Hamza Petrika.

Only a few men who worked behind the barbed wire and plank fencing of the conversation area could enter the village by special permission, and each wore his name on a dog tag dangling from a chain around his neck. In the winter, even though they were inoculated now and again, these forest dwellers often fell victim to the recurring epidemic, and if one of them strayed off and stretched out in the brush, never to rise again, that inscribed tag came in very handy. The banks of the Sinistra were flanked by ancient wild forests, so the dead weren't always found quickly.

There was only one clinic in the Dobrin forest district, and when news spread that Colonel Puiu Borcan had been felled by the Tungusic Flu, the doctor's courtyard was overrun by lumberjacks, road workers, mushroom hunters, and, of course, bear wardens. Each demanded an inoculation. They waited there in front of the closed clinic for four or five days on end, sitting about on the verandah steps or on the rocks scattered about the yard; the luckier ones, though even they looked increasingly pale and sickly, got spots at the foot of the fence, which was painted all over with red crosses. From inside, the medical orderlies peered nervously out from behind gauze curtains. One of them—wearing a tattered, soiled white smock over pale green army trousers, and with sandals on his bare feet that revealed nails brown with dirt, long pointy toenails that resembled griffin claws—occasionally stepped out onto the threshold to call upon everyone waiting outside for patience. By way of excuse, he invariably said that the time for inoculations was not yet officially here, and yet late autumn was no doubt upon them: the silvery steam of all those men breathing in the yard hovered about in the bright sunshine.

Toward evening on the fourth or fifth day, along with the dispiriting lights of dusk, the gray ganders all at once arrived and told everyone to go home. These were Coca Mavrodin's men: long-necked, button-eyed figures with light tufts of spider's web hair around their ears, thin, transparent skin, and not a wrinkle on their faces. They really did look like geese.

The ganders announced that everyone should go on home in peace since this winter would be epidemic-free, and there would be no need for inoculations. After coaxing the medical orderlies out of the clinic, the gray ganders went inside and personally brought the boxes full of medicine out to the yard, stomping to bits every last one of them. All those glass vials crackling under their feet sent the sour vaccine smell wafting over the fences of nearby homes, descending onto the plum trees and stacks of hay in the yards, and mixing with the damp odor of forest mold.

This was good news: the game wardens dispersed along with all those other, not particularly sociable characters of the same stripe, all of them practically tiptoeing away, a bit embarrassed with relief. And yet the rustle of rubber boots treading along the dewy trails that led up the mountain slopes did not die down so fast. Everyone left except for Géza Kökény—he, of whom it was said that no illness could catch him—smoking his Pope there at the bottom of the steps.

I too now headed off along the dark main road, at the end of which loomed the lights of the train station. Before getting far from the clinic, though, I met up with Doc Oleinek, the chief bear warden, and one of the two Hamza Petrikas. Doc was my occasional drinking buddy, whom I recognized first on account of his smell as he trudged along in front of me—though not the smell of medicine (he was a doc in name alone, for he spent all his time tending to the bears). He had a wild, nauseating smell, like a bush pissed on for days, weeks, months. Sixty or seventy bears—or one hundred and sixty, one hundred and seventy?— were kept in abandoned mines and in a ramshackle old chapel in the conservation area, and were looked after by my friend and the albino twins.

Doc Oleinek offered to buy me a drink, and as we were making our way toward the station along that soft, silent, dewy road, all at once I noticed the feather grass hair of one of the Hamza Petrikas lit up not far away. He'd of course been walking with Doc, though like some sort of toy poodle, slinking along behind at a proper distance. The other Hamza Petrika had evidently stayed behind in the woods, with the bears.

A narrow-gauge railway led to the reserve, and that's how fodder was delivered to the bears. And until the first snowfall, those few men who worked there would go into Dobrin City on a handcar.

A hurricane lamp hung from the eaves of the loading platform, and a bunch of people were waiting under its hazy orb of yellow light. Every night on the branch line from Sinistra a train arrived that comprised two third-class passenger cars together with a freight car. Once a week, on Sunday nights, a load of denatured alcohol arrived with the other cargo, and a portion of that was distributed on the spot, though of course only to those authorized to receive it. Doc Oleinek fished the alcohol ration coupons out of his bag, pressed them into Hamza Petrika's palm, and told him to go stand in line and redeem them as soon as the train pulled in.

Denatured alcohol—strained through bread, spongy mushrooms, or crushed blueberries—is the favorite drink up in these woods. If no blueberries or bolete mushrooms happen to be available, a bit of a sock will also do. Or a handful of earth.

From the other side of the main station a narrow-gauge railway led toward the conservation area, which meant having to make one's way past the purple lights of the switches and over the dewy glow of the tracks. It wound its way along the plank fence of the lumberyard and out of the village. To render the frequent burglaries a bit harder to pull off, each plank had been sharpened at the top not long before, and in the mist of distant lights they now gave off a honeyed sparkle. Below them was the handcar, chained to the bumper that marked the end of the tracks. Doc Oleinek and I sat down on the handcar and watched for the evening train, whose rattling could already be heard as it made its way over distant bridges, its whistles resounding between the Sinistra Valley's steep walls.

"They've postponed the epidemic," observed Doc Oleinek.

"Yeah."

"You believe that?"

"Why not."

Whenever a strange mood got hold of me and I didn't feel like talking, there was no shaking me out of it. This would have been the perfect opportunity to start firing away questions about things up in the conservation area—maybe he knew something about Béla Bundasian, my adopted son, that I would never find out otherwise—but it felt better to keep quiet.

Rather than forcing a conversation, Doc tucked himself into that bear smell of his. We were drinking buddies who plied our pastime in silence. Rare moments came along, though, when we'd exchange an indifferent, empty word or half-sentence, but for the most part we expressed companionship by clearing our throats. When Hamza Petrika could be heard approaching, however, the bottles knocking against each other in his satchel, the chief bear warden sprang up and ran to meet him.

"Listen here," he said in a hushed, somewhat muffled but still almost warm tone of voice: "I'm letting you go—you can be on your way right this instant."

"You're joking."

"No, I'm not. Before you know it, we'll catch something from each other. You heard it with your own ears—there are no more inoculations. It's best if we part ways, if everyone tends to his own affairs."

"I couldn't take a step without you, Doc. My brother and I want to stay with you forever. If you're afraid, then we'll hide away for a while and promise not to come near, and we'll wait till you get over this."

"No, I've made up my mind—but I promise I won't report anything to the gray ganders until you've had a good head start."

And Doc Oleinek, to drive his point home, took a bottle out of the satchel, the one that must have been meant for Hamza Petrika, and set it on the ground in front of him. Then he turned on his heel and got back up beside me on the handcar. From there he shouted this:

"Drink as much as you can, and then get lost. Come morning, once you're out of sight, I'll file a report."

Hamza Petrika must have known this side of Doc Oleinek, for he no longer tried pleading with him: he sat down on the embankment and starting swigging. Doc too flicked the sheet-metal cap off his bottle, and we got down to drinking. There were neither mushrooms nor blueberries on hand that night, so we strained the alcohol through the cuff of his jacket.

A deep, damp, sticky silence descended on the valley, broken only now and again by the hooting of an owl from somewhere near all those boards stacked up beyond the fence or by a farm dog barking; later we could hear that three-car train roll slowly back out of the station and then away down the sloping track toward Sinistra. There were the occasional blubbering sobs of Hamza Petrika: amid rapid gurgles he sniffled loudly like an offended, squeamish little dog. Albinos, I thought to myself, must be weak-nerved beings who easily go mad.

Doc Oleinek asked me obligingly: "Doesn't my smell bother you?" He no doubt hoped to break the silence that had perhaps ensued precisely on account of that smell. "Come on, be honest. I know I stink a little."

"Not at all."

"Oh, come on—I know I've had a few crazy incidents."

"You smell totally fine."

"Don't try conning me. Women have ditched me, one after another. And they've told me, too, that it's because I stink. I'm not saying I was so crazy about them, either. Anyway, then the twins were stationed with me."

"There are lots of good things about twins."

"That's true. Twins are dainty. The three of us brought each other lots of joy—we lived up there like a happy little family. But that's over now. Your health, that's what counts." Getting up from the handcar, he sounded practically relieved as he yelled over to Hamza Petrika, "You hear me?! And you know, there's such a thing as good manners—you might at least thank me before heading on your way."

But where, minutes ago, Hamza Petrika's guttural, childlike sobs could be heard, only the stones of the embankment stirred. Where the albino bear warden had been, an opaque darkness hovered, a blackness that had no one within it, that was completely empty.

Doc Oleinek now walked over, kicking his feet about the area thick with trash and clumps of weeds living and dried-out. Along the way he happened to kick up an empty bottle and, finally, returned with a pair of rubber boots.

"His," he grumbled, repeatedly taking deep sniffs. "But what came over him? Why'd he take them off? Where the fuck could he have gone barefoot?"

He sat back on the handcar, and we went on taking gulps of the denatured alcohol after straining it through the cuff of his jacket. After a while Doc lay back comfortably enough, and I too, in a bit of a stupor, stretched out on the plank seat. Then, all at once, we simultaneously noticed a single match flare out above the pile of wood boards beyond the fence, then the embers of a cigarette glowing, fading, glowing again. Like some mysterious black hole, Hamza Petrika's silhouette was suddenly in the sky blocking out the stars. He was camped out up high, having a smoke.

"Hid yourself, huh," Doc Oleinek shouted over to him. "We were getting awfully worried about what became of you—my friend here was even a bit offended at your leaving without having said good-bye." And because Hamza Petrika did not reply, he quickly added, "And why didn't you offer us something from your secret tobacco stash?"

"Because," came Hamza Petrika's curt rejoinder.

That one-word response sounded like a pocket watch splashing at night into a black silent stream. Before long the cigarette fell out of his hand into the weeds, flickering there like a firefly.

"Hmm."

Doc Oleinek got up and went to look for the butt. On finding it, he slipped it into a cigarette holder, then the two of us kept passing it calmly back and forth until we'd smoked all there was to smoke.

"Yes indeed," grumbled Doc, "these damn twins. That's how they are. Tear them apart from each other for a couple of hours and they get into all kinds of trouble. Who the hell knows what to make of them?"

Indeed, Doc must have been a bit mystified, for while still sitting there on the edge of the handcar, he kept calling out to Hamza Petrika. Getting no reply, he placed the rubber boots on the seat and headed over to the fence. He walked up and down before finally grabbing one of the planks and shaking it in irritation: "Hey!"

And when, after a little while, he finally let it go, his fingers parted from the wood with a sort of sticky sound, as if from glue—or fresh blood.

Getting back on the handcar, Doc Oleinek gave a furious huff and spat out a big glob and then wiped his palms on the seat. He found the bottle and, now without a bit of caution, took a swig before extending it toward me.

"Take a good fast plug yourself," he whispered. "Then let's

get out of here. I think the boy has impaled himself."

"What the hell does that mean?"

"What do you think? He looks for the hole in his ass, nudges the pointy end of the post inside, and—wham!—sits right down."

"I can't believe it."

"Believe it or not, but come on, let's get out of here."

Freeing the handcar's chain from the bumper, releasing the brakes, and grabbing the handle, Doc took off in no time. But Hamza Petrika stayed right there atop the fence, his silhouette blocking the stars while purple orbs of light glimmered below from the switches.

"It would be best if I take you along with me for a stretch," said Doc. "We should stick together for a while."

"Fine," I said. "How about taking me down to my friend Colonel Jean Tomoioaga's guard booth?

"Sure, and meanwhile we'll guzzle down what's left in the bottle. Or do you have a better idea?"

"Nothing comes to mind just now."

"Same here—and let's get as far away from here as possible."

"But Doc, how do they get him off that fence?"

"They don't," Doc replied angrily. "Can't be done. If you get hold of his feet, after all, you'd just wind up driving it in deeper."

"I just wondered."

"Don't bother—it's his business, and we don't have the right to meddle. Don't even think of it again. Though you can keep talking to some of them, by the way, for days afterward."

Leaving the station, it took us some hard seesawing, as the tracks began their steep ascent, to roll our way out of the village. The screeching of the wheels shot right up the tracks, announcing our presence, and before we knew it, the barking of dogs undulated in waves all along the embankment and up the mountainside.

Along the way, I asked, "Does this means a position has opened up at your place?"

"Maybe even two."

"I'd go to the woods with you," I went on. "I could have a word with that lieutenant colonel, the medical orderly, about pulling some strings and maybe getting me an inoculation after all. If it's okay with you, I'd gladly like to go. I'm not saying I know much about bears, but I could learn."

"I wouldn't get your hopes up."

"But, all the same, maybe I could come?"

"We'll see. For now, I'd like to be on my own for a while."

I accompanied Doc Oleinek on the handcar as far as the entrance to the conservation area, where a crossing gate topped by a red lit hurricane lamp closed the tracks. In the guard's room lived my old chess-playing pal, Colonel Jean Tomoioaga. Setting out, I'd counted on whiling away a bit of time at his place; drinking a bit, and that I'd amble back down to the village in the middle of the night on my own two feet.

The hurricane lamp soon found its way to the threshold, where Colonel Jean Tomoioaga switched its red lens to white, and then got out the chessboard. We played with ungainly, little home-made figures on a checkered shirt he laid out on the floor. The whole thing could be swept up in a moment—the mountain infantrymen did not take kindly to games.

In no particular hurry himself, Doc Oleinek also took a seat near the doorway and the lamp, watching us to line up the pieces, not in a mood to go on just yet.

"I see you're going back on your own," Jean Tomoioaga said to him. "Our friend Hamsa got a little extra leave?"

"Well, I let him go."

From underneath his plank bed Jean Tomoioaga took out a bottle and set it on the floor in easy reach. Tossing about inside was the bluish-gray fluid of denatured alcohol filtered through wood coal—it's said that coal is healthy.

"And when is he returning, if I may ask? You know I have to record every movement in my log."

"If he comes, then he does, and you can write whatever you need to write. If he doesn't come, you don't have to write a thing."

"You're a character."

Colonel Jean Tomoioaga and I were on our second or third game when, in front of the door, against the black velvet of the valley, Hamza Petrika's feather grass hair flared up. Not the Hamza Petrika who'd impaled himself, but the other one. He stood by the open door, bloomy and glistening with little droplets of dew, without a trace of blood scent about him.

"Where is he?" he asked Doc Oleinek seriously.

"You can see for yourself that he's not here."

"I want to speak with my brother right away."

"You can't, not now."

Hands in his pockets, he just stood there by the door and, glancing behind us, gazed around the little guard room.

"I see you brought his boots with you, Doc. So why should I ask where my brother's feet wound up?" And he pointed a finger at me. "Say, is he going to fill our shoes by any chance?"

"The future will decide that," said Doc. "But as long as you're starting to catch on, listen up: you too can take off. You're free, so get going. Somewhere, who knows where, your brother, Hamza Petrika, is waiting for you. I promised him that I wouldn't have them start searching for you right away."

Hamza Petrika sat down on the ground and ran his fingers through his hair, which was so feathery that his hand stayed empty. He spit into his palm, then smoothed down his hair. After that, he got up and stretched. His face suddenly smoothed out; he was calm.

"All right, Doc. I'm off; I'll go pack up our things. But you promise not to come right after me."

"If that's what you want, fine. For how long? Will twenty minutes do? Or maybe a half-hour?"

"That's exactly what I had in mind. That's how long I'd like to be completely alone."

"Okay, you're all right—take your time."

Without a word Hamza Petrika tucked his brother's rubber boots under his arm and started back toward the bear reserve, letting out colossal farts on the way, as if his soul was fast departing his body. He'd gone only a few steps, though, when the murmur of the brook and the velvet darkness closed in behind him.

Doc Oleinek, not that he had a watch, waited generously. Surely twice as much time had passed as he'd promised when he began to stretch. Listlessly he slung the satchel full of bottles onto his shoulder and headed toward the handcar.

"Good seeing you."

"Please," I called after him, "think about it."

"All right, all right, we'll see."

A bit later I headed off, too, ambling down along the embankment toward Dobrin City. Some people are soothed by walking on railroad ties, some are irritated, and others are driven to reflection. I simply got it into my head that on reaching the edge of the village, rather than heading for the Baba Rotunda Pass, I'd take a detour to the station, where perhaps I could exchange a few words with Hamza Petrika. What sort of words, I had no idea, but something was sure to come up. Nothing did come of this chitchat however, after all.

By daybreak I reached the station. The sky had started to turn yellow in the distance, above the purple contours of the pass, and with each step I waited for Hamza Petrika's scarecrow silhouette to loom large against the sky. I went all along the fence but found him nowhere. Sitting in a row on the loading platform, dangling their legs and stretching their necks, were the gray ganders.

At the spot where Hamza Petrika had lit a cigarette the previous evening, half of one of the fence posts was missing, sawed off about waist high. A thick layer of fragrant sawdust covered the ground at its base. A sole competing smell was in the sharp early morning breeze—a bit metallic, a tad salty and a tad sweet, exactly like blood.

It was getting light, but I figured that rather than try to get some rest I'd go look up the lieutenant colonel who served as medical orderly—maybe he'd really do me a favor. Getting that inoculation was my big opportunity to settle into life as a bear warden.

9

CONNIE ILLAFELD'S HAIR

One fine spring day, back when I worked as an assistant corpse watchman, I finally got to know Connie Illafeld—it wasn't exactly the most delightful meeting I'd ever had, seeing as how, for all practical purposes, she no longer spoke any one single language. Instead she mixed them left and right, and the only people who could communicate with her somewhat had to know Ukrainian, Swabian German, Romanian, and Hungarian, and it didn't hurt to know Carpathian German and Ruthenian dialects as well. Few such people lived in the Dobrin forest district, but one of them happened to be the chief bear warden, my friend Doc Oleinek.

Connie Illafeld was a sort of pen name. The progeny of the Illarions—landowning, serf-holding Bukovinian boyars—this woman, who lived among simple mountain folk on her family's onetime estate, had originally been named Cornelia Illarion. Perhaps some other person around there might conceivably have been known as either Cornelia Illarion or Connie Illafeld, one person alone could lay claim to both these appellations.

So when I happened to notice one day the name *Cornelia Illarion* on a file folder emblazoned with the Red Cross—a folder destined for the clerk's desk—and that this name was followed by her pen name in a flourish of red and in quotes. I knew it was her—practically a relative of mine, my adopted son's onetime lover. I was dying of curiosity: I had to see for myself the being who, years earlier, had stoked the wild side of Béla Bundasian.

Back then I was working for the Dobrin mountain infantry as a civilian non-staff member; alongside various secret commissions small and large, I was the deputy to the district coroner or, as the locals put it, the assistant corpse watchman. The morgue stood in a musty old corner of the barracks, and when it rang of emptiness—which is to say, when there was no work—I assisted Colonel Titus Tomoioaga in the office. Since the district fully belonged to the mountain infantry, he was the one who kept records on everyone dispatched to Dobrin and who sent all the new arrivals to work. He was a slow, dreamy, mountain infantryman with the soul of an elk, however, who would stare listlessly out the window at the birds and at the gray clouds passing by over the spruces and firs. For him, reading even the most curtly worded records was a challenge.

On the day in question, the first warm breeze had just tumbled over the southern ranges' icy ridges—a breeze packed with heavy scents. Flower petals and willow catkin pollen hovered above the streambed: word had it that among the Old Believers it was Easter. With spring two new internees came to Dobrin.

When, dizzy from the bright sunshine and the pollen, I stepped into the dimly lit office and there saw Cornelia Illarion's name on a Red Cross file folder, I thought I was imagining things. Yet there was her pen name too, its letters finely hatched, all this on the Red Cross-emblazoned folder—lifting its cover revealed that the individual concerned had been sent here from the Colonia Sinistra sanatorium.

I'd always been a levelheaded, disciplined fellow, but uneasiness suddenly beset me. And, though this wasn't at all the custom in Dobrin, I started to gently pump Colonel Titus Tomoio-aga for information. What did he know? How did this woman wind up here? Who was she?

"Oh, she's no one," grumbled the colonel a bit drowsily. "We got her from the Yellows. They're the ones who sent her here, out of the kindness of their hearts. But if you're actually interested in her, well then, you'll get to know her in just a moment when you record her data."

So that's how things stood. Colonia Sinistra was a famous sanatorium. Even people who'd never been there knew its buildings were painted yellow and glowed at night. Among ourselves we referred to the institution's administrators and attendants as "the Yellows."

"And what's the plan? Do you know where you're placing her?"

"More or less. Colonel Coca Mavrodin-Mahmudia wants her sent to the bears right away. True, she's not in the best shape, she babbles away in all sorts of languages like a madwoman, but Doc Oleinek will manage somehow."

So, Coca Mavrodin was sending Connie Illafeld to the bear reserve.

It must have been clear as day on my face that I didn't receive this news exactly with indifference. "This will all be for the best, you'll see," Colonel Titus Tomoioaga added reassuringly: "Doc speaks all languages, so he'll no doubt be able to communicate with her."

Before being taken into treatment, Connie Illafeld had lived in an alpine village, her house at the upper end of Punte Sinistra, near the watershed, beside the train station. It wasn't a genuine station, though, just a stopping place, a sidetrack next to the rail line, where the trains ascending the mountain from either side would rest, take on water, and wait out each other's scheduled arrivals. Just up the slope, the tracks disappeared into a tunnel, which let out purple puffs of thick smoke for hours after a train passed through; the north side of Connie Illafeld's house had seen its share of soot over the years.

Connie Illafeld, the pen name of this last member of the Illarion family, lived as a recluse and made her living by painting everyday scenes from antiquity on small, pocket-size plates of glass; she worked on commission for Jews from Chernivtsi and Lviv, though how she managed to get them across the border to the Ukraine was a mystery. She was at least forty, her eyes were green, her skin was white, and her hair was black.

Forest rangers, road workers, and professional hunters passing through sometimes hit on her, of course, but by all appearances she was saving herself for someone. The tunnel watchman, who never slept, claimed that a foreign traveler was wooing her—a fellow from Galicia who supposedly swam across the Tisza River every night and who sometimes paid her a secret visit, too. But that was only a sleepless watchman's story: everyone knew that an impenetrable barbed-wire border fence stretched along the riverbank. Regardless, even if Connie Illafeld had had a secret someone, she sent him packing that spring, when her true love appeared on the scene: Béla Bundasian, my adopted son.

One night the intercity slow train pulled into the Punte Sinistra station, and Béla Bundasian got off without his bag for a quick drink from a spring bubbling near the tracks. As he leaned over to quench his thirst, his shirt slipped up his back and his jacket collar fell over his neck, covering his ears, and so he didn't hear the little trembling of the stones under the railroad ties as the train went on without him. Since the tracks descended in both directions from the Punte station, the engineers had only to release the brakes to get a train rolling on its own. That day, for some reason, the intercity train did not wait for its counterpart coming from the other direction to arrive, and so when my adopted son straightened up to wipe the water from his lips, he had just a second to notice the last car vanish into the tunnel.

Only one intercity train plied this route daily, and if such an inadvertently abandoned passenger wanted to stick to his plans, he had no choice but to wait until the next evening.

It was spring—Palm Sunday or something along those lines. The air was rich with heady fragrances, and even after sunset dizzying bird warbles streamed from the black forests of looming spruce and fir. Busily cleaning the window, Connie Illafeld was kneeling on the sill in a rolled-up skirt, her white arm lit up in the dusk. No doubt even the sound of the wet paper slipping across the glass might have been inviting, and Béla Bundasian must have planted himself by the front gate like someone come to serve notice.

Did Connie Illafeld sense which way the wind was blowing? No doubt she did. Her hand slowed on the window, and one could see through her sweet slightly parted lips her sharp white teeth as well as the unbridled bliss of her glowing green eyes—all of this was directed at my adopted son. Being half Armenian, Béla Bundasian was parchment-hued, the whites of his eyes were a tad oily, and his eyebrows were already quite bushy, and so at first glance he might well have met with the approval of just about any woman. Well aware of this, he wasted no time, playing up the role as the hapless, left-behind traveler. He'd been on his way to the paper mill in the city of Putna to get sheet music paper, when he'd had the bad luck—or was it now?—to get off the train for a drink of water. That this was indeed what had happened, Connie Illafeld could see for herself, so she invited him in to have some rest. If by chance he was still thirsty, she said, she had a bucket full of water, so he could drink to his heart's content.

Seeing that the floor of the house was covered by a soft, thick woolen blanket, Béla Bundasian tactfully left his shoes on the threshold. So he was in his socks when he happened to step on

Connie Illafeld's bare feet. And since that felt good, he left his feet right there. The heady smell of pasta emanated from the walls, from the handcrafted rustic furniture, from the handwoven fabrics. Connie Illafeld smelled of pasta, too—her downy underarms and her pearly thighs—and even though she was old enough to have been Béla Bundasian's mother, this scent of unbridled desire welled up out of her as if from a loaf of bread rising in the oven. In a matter of minutes they were pawing each other like mad.

In one of her drawers Connie Illafeld kept a dried herb—the flowers, leaves, and crumbled stems of sweet woodruff. She now sprinkled this concoction all over the woolen blanket, and within intoxicating fragrance the two of them lolled about nonstop for two or three weeks, fogging her windows up with the vapors of true passion. Much later—by which time everything was long over—I peered into Béla Bundasian's diary, which had chronicled those weeks and months of love. That's how I know all this. He wrote that getting his fill of her was impossible, it only took a glance at her and he'd be overwhelmed with the sensation that lurking even between her toes was a hungry little pussy, so it was best to just gulp the whole of her down like a glass of water. And yet—by a secret, circuitous route—the end of the love affair was of course already at hand.

Back in those days I rarely saw my adopted son. When he traveled to Moldavia for sheet music paper—his occupation involved copying scores—he'd vanish for weeks on end. As fond as I was of the boy, I let him do whatever he wanted, figuring that he wasn't my own blood, after all, and could go through his baptism by fire: I resolved to intervene only in an extreme situation.

And that time finally came. During one of his extended absences, a stranger came in the form of a gray-haired gentleman with yellow eyes and a narrow mouth who left a package wrapped in newspapers and tied up with string. No sooner had this gray-haired man left than I opened the bundle. It held note-book pages written in Polish: a mimeograph. I naturally burned them at once, mixing the ashes in water and pouring them all over the garden. At that point, however, it didn't matter one bit. Béla Bundasian had gotten mixed up in something.

After the Polish notebooks incident, my adopted son never showed up again. Granted, I'd suspected from the start that something was up, but where could I have searched for him?

I boarded the intercity train to Moldavia, and after one night of travel in bone-chilling cold and the dizzying smell of coal smoke, I arrived in Punta Sinistra. The wind died down by eve-ning and the warm scent of hay rose from the barns and settled over the surrounding rimy meadows.

And yet it wasn't a particularly pleasant feeling that came over me—no, in the light of the train cars rolling away toward the tunnel I noticed immediately that Connie Illafeld's door was fes-tooned with official-looking stamps and that a Red Cross ribbon hung from the knob—anyone visited by the Red Cross could not be in good straights. The Red Cross on a door or a gate was a clear sign that something was wrong, terribly wrong.

Not that the tunnel watchman was in an especially talkative mood, but he did say this much: Cornelia Illarion had indeed lived in the house over there. Yes, *lived*, not lives. In fact, hardly a couple of days or weeks earlier, two gentleman had come with official papers declaring her insane. And they had taken her off to that renowned asylum, Colonia Sinistra, right away.

As for my adopted son, Béla Bundasian, I finally met up with him here in the Dobrin forest district only four years later, in the house of the meteorologist, Géza Hutira. It turned out that on the same day that Cornelia Illarion was taken away, his longtime benefactor, Colonel Velman, was waiting for him by the evening train. The colonel was an unsolicited, uninvited good friend who at times assumed the role of confidential well-wisher by looking Béla Bundasian up and providing him with various sorts of advice. On this occasion the Colonel didn't mention the Polish notebooks, but warned that he could count on some unpleasant consequences on account of his dubious romantic dealings. Word had it that he'd been spending lots of time in the provinces of late—sleeping in the home of a female individual unaccountable for her own actions—he may have been in Connie Illafeld's bed—and this was very close to what the law called rape. He, as Béla Bundasian's longtime benefactor, would try his best to smooth things over, so maybe he'd be let off easy, with just a couple years of internment.

This was all I knew about Connie Illafeld when I saw her name on that file folder, but soon enough I spread her documents out in front of me. All these details—nice and slow—went through my mind as I sat there, accompanied by the fact that the woman had wound up among the bears on the reserve at the behest of Colonel Coca Mavrodin.

Béla Bundasian lived there, too, but way higher up, above the tree line, at the meteorologist's place. He'd learned to read the instruments and the weather vanes and even during holidays or when he got leave every six months or so, he never budged from there. At most he would pay a visit to the bear wardens to play dice, nine-men's morris, and blackjack.

"You'll see, this will all be for the best," said Colonel Titus Tomoioaga.

"But still," I began, and then paused, unsure of what to say.

"What is it," Colonel Titus Tomoioaga asked, now looking me over suspiciously. "What's your problem?"

"Nothing."

Once again I glanced at the folder, then asked for permission to go to the restroom, which was at the end of the hallway. Of course I was full of curiosity to see her for myself—my adopted son's enchantress, this stunning woman I'd often imagined, that zesty little dish who, as I read Béla Bundasian's diary, without ever having actually seen her, I'd almost coveted for myself.

Success was not in the cards. I opened the door to the hallway and saw, on the bench where people waited to be called inside, a gray-skinned, coughing, slumping, stretched-out fellow in a miner's helmet. Beside him was a figure cloaked in a threadbare quilted jacket, praying away, whose clasped hands and face were almost completely covered by a knotted mass of hair.

"Listen," I said, turning back to Colonel Titus Tomoioaga, "I don't know what sort of woman we're talking about. There's not a single lady waiting out there—maybe she took off?"

"She's there, all right."

"There's only a miner sprawled out on the bench along with another fellow with hair all over him. No one except them."

"Well, but she's there, in any case."

Connie Illafeld was indeed waiting in the hallway. Colonel Titus Tomoioaga soon summoned her. At first he called her name, but then he realized that maybe she wouldn't take that in, so he stepped out into the hallway and, placing a hand under one of her arms, helped her inside. It was the hairy figure.

From between the strands of silky black hair that covered her face her green eyes glowed. She did not know her own name. Trying my best to be good-humored about the situation, I sought out Colonel Titus Tomoioaga's eyes to exchange a knowing glance. And I even forced a smile or two, as one often does in the presence of a person not quite right in the head.

"People forget everything in there," explained Colonel Titus Tomoioaga, "everything trickles out of a person, like shit."

"But to not even remember her name ..."

"Well, maybe that's not all bad."

"And maybe you see things differently ... but I for one think there's a little too much hair on her."

"It is a fact," said Colonel Titus Tomoioaga, "that she had very thorough treatment. They must have overdosed her on something. I wouldn't be surprised if maybe something else even grew on her."

"You mean a weenie?"

"Yep . . . and maybe someone will go looking for it."

Once I'd finished the paperwork, Colonel Titus Tomoioaga asked me to escort the prospective bear warden to the metal shop, where one of those little sheet-metal dog tags would be hung around her neck, too.

But just then, Doc Oleinek, the chief bear warden, who supposedly spoke all possible languages, stopped by the office. In no time he engaged Connie Illafeld in a conversation of sorts, and it seemed they quickly understood each other. In the end he was the one who accompanied her to the metal shop.

"I can tell you're worried," said Colonel Titus Tomoioaga. "You're worried about something, but let me reassure you it's not necessary—this individual will be in good hands."

"To hell with it all," I spat out, recklessly again.

"Hey, what's the matter?"

"Nothing, I swear."

When Connie Illarion returned to the office at Doc Oleinek's side, she wore a shiny metal nameplate on her hairy neck, one that hung from a brand new chain whose end had been welded shut so no one could ever remove it again. There was no denying that the name—once that of a seductress—was now worn by an animal.

Before they left, Doc Oleinek—my old drinking buddy—devoted a couple of minutes to me as well. It was from him that I learned that same morning, my adopted son, Béla Bundasian, had been given a day off even though it wasn't due him. They had come down from the conservation area on the handcar, and now he was drinking up at the station, where denatured alcohol had been handed out to the forest rangers.

"Come along with us if you want to meet up with him," said Doc Oleinek. "You can have a shot or two together. Today is

Easter among the Old Believers."

"No," I replied. "I'm not in the mood today."

"Maybe you've got a message for him."

"No, at the moment I've got nothing to say."

Doc Oleinek now headed down the hallway, the hairy Connie Illafeld following along behind like a lapdog, the sheet-metal nameplate swinging from her neck. Once they were out in the yard, in the sun, it began to glitter against the walls, the trees. It was brand new. From now on, anyone who saw her would know just who they were dealing with. They were on their way to the narrow-gauge railway station, where my adopted son, Béla Bundasian, was waiting by the handcar.

Before long I got booted from my corpse-watching job. And on the morning I had to hand over my position to my successor, Toni Tescovina, as I was about to show him the tricks of the trade, I found the body of Connie Illafeld, alias Cornelia Illarion, spread out on the gray stone table. The blood on her neck—where someone had ripped off her dog tag with no little violence—was dark blue, like clotted blueberry juice or, like the blood of the Illarions, Ruthenian boyars. By the time she wound up in there, her clothes, stiff from grime, had been cut right off her in the morgue, and when I chanced to touch her, she felt colder than the stone table she was on. Having lost its shine, like some sort of blackened hoarfrost, her hair peeled off her with a hushed rustle until finally, once that operation was complete, there she lay, buck naked, before us.

"Where do you wash up?" asked Toni Tescovina on the way out. "I'm on my way to the square. Géza Kökény mentioned on the way over that tomorrow is Easter. And I'm all covered with hair."

"Damn it," I grumbled. "I've had a bit too much of Easter. And as for the hair, you'd better get used to it. It's a hairy job."

10

GÉZA HUTIRA'S EAR

That year the coldest day came at the start of spring. The night before, when the fire died down and the valley's cold slithered down the chimney into the cabin, Géza Hutira could no longer sleep. Instead he tried to keep Bebe Tescovina warm. For a while he held her tight in his lap, and then after covering her with every old rag at hand, he arranged her, lying down on himself, and covering her with his hair and even his beard. Although he did doze off for a bit, he could hear even while half-asleep a scraping and squeaking of snow from the valley: someone was approaching along the frozen, silent streambed. Before long the stamping of feet had reached the threshold, and when Géza Hutira shone his flashlight upon the hoarfrost-coated figure—with gleaming tusks of ice hanging from its his nostrils which were issuing comet-like puffs of steam—he recognized him as Nikifor Tescovina, and Géza thought he'd come to take his child home.

But the commissary manager didn't so much as glance at his daughter. He was looking for Géza Hutira.

"Get something warm on, now," said Nikifor Tescovina. "And make sure you've got some tobacco, something to chew on. We're headed off for a couple of days."

"I don't leave home much in the middle of the night," grumbled Géza Hutira. "And it's never happened that I haven't read my instruments on time. Who do you think will register the measurements for me?"

"Oh, come on—you know full well that no one gives a shit about those observations of yours."

"If I must go, then which way, where?"

"They'll tell us."

When on the threshold they'd tied on their snowshoes only the snow still shone. The meteorologist's house was above the tree line, so it was in the open that the two men now trudged their way up the mountainside and crossed a narrow plateau before descending down the other side into the Baba Rotunda Pass. Waiting for them in the road worker Andrei's cabin was Colonel Coca Mavrodin of the Dobrin mountain infantry.

"We're off to visit the sick," she announced when her two men arrived: "We'll look around the Kolinda forest a bit, where the retired forest rangers live. Word has it that they're not in great shape. Indeed, health-wise I can only report the worst. Let's go see what we can do for them."

Stretched out at the foot of the Kolinda forest was a tiny village of towering snowdrifts, shaped by the wind from the slopes, and looming between its scattered sun-faded and fog-washed houses. Once they arrived there, the jeep skidding and floundering along, finally came to a halt in front of a small wooden church at the end of the road. Lolling about on the verandah of the parsonage, leaning on his elbow, was a pale young man, the parish priest: Father Pantelimon. Out in the yard, blanketed in fog, were three black horses.

Rather than wearing his usual vestment, the priest was dressed like anyone else around here or, more precisely, like the mountain infantrymen: a black vinyl jacket over a roughly knit grass-green wool sweater; threadbare military trousers; and sandals on his bare feet. Not even in the kitchen did the snow melt off his naked toes.

"You've got to wait a bit," he said, "the fellow hasn't gotten here yet. Maybe he got held up along the way." He then unfolded the newspaper-wrapped package in his hands to reveal a few half-frozen boiled potatoes, a couple of onions, and some withered apples: "Something to keep your bellies going—who knows when you'll be done."

Walking down the well-trodden purple snowy path, past thick steam swirling above the horses, he now crossed the yard toward the open sacristy. From inside came a sound reminiscent of a distant reed organ: the creaking of a door. But the wind swept through the yard, seizing every trace of that sound.

It was the coldest day of the year, but the door to the kitchen stayed wide open all the same, with only the rainbow-hued curtain of steam fluttering before it. From the cracked walls came the cold smell of mice along with the sound of plaster being scratched at and crumbling. The table was covered by a sticky tablecloth of waxed linen, with a nine-men's morris board drawn in indelible pencil in the middle. Reaching in a pocket of her greatcoat, Colonel Coca Mavrodin produced the black and white pieces and lined them up on the edge of the table.

Returning from the sacristy, Father Pantelimon brought saddles—carrying two on his shoulders and dragging one behind him in the snow. Throwing them over the horses' backs, he tightened the girth under their bellies. The bird shit that dotted the shoulder of his vinyl jacket sparkled like a colonel's stars. As for the two colonels themselves, for the time being they just sat in silence at the kitchen table playing nine-men's morris. The door was wide open all the while. Out in the bitter cold, the horses stamped their hooves while sparrows and crows occasionally landed on their fresh, steaming hot manure.

It was past noon by the time a snowmobile arrived through

the snowdrifts with a great roar—the sort of fast, narrow contraption used by the Dobrin mountain infantry. This one was driven not by a soldier, however, but by a man in a quilted jacket, a lambskin cap, and rubber boots. On the threshold he left behind a saddlebag that, from the sound of it, was packed full of glass bottles. No sooner had he arrived than he turned the snowmobile around and drove off.

The bottles must have been corked in a hurry, for the scent of cheap rum flooded the kitchen in no time. Father Pantelimon poured equal amounts of the drink into two plastic containers, meanwhile asking the two men, who were helping him, not to so much as lick their fingers afterward.

The saddlebag, now bearing the plastic containers, wound up on the pommel of one of the saddles. Then all three—the two men and Colonel Coca Mavrodin—got on the horses. Chewing on a matchstick, the priest looked after them from the verandah of the parsonage as they rode the beasts out of the village on a narrow, well-trodden trail.

Coca Mavrodin asked her two men to proceed Indian file if possible, and always only on the right side of the trail, so as to cut a clearly visible groove through the snow. The Kolinda forest covered an amorphous, hulking beast of a mountain whose plateau-like summit sprawled out flat, far, and wide amid other, taller ranges. The Baba Rotunda Pass, though hardly an hour or two away, always seemed to hover in brownish wisps of fog on the eastern horizon. The forest covered even the top of the mountain, its slopes consequently featured not a lacework of snowy meadows but instead only a few odd rectangular clear cuts which shone brightly in the sun.

Not even by afternoon did the freeze let up. Half-frozen crows perched on rimy spruces, looking like enormous cones against the gray sky. Frigid water pearls took shape on Coca Mavrodin's wool-felt greatcoat each time she exhaled, and whenever one of the horses broke wind, a comet of hot steam hissed forth from its behind.

The trail hardly ascended, and they had to follow the muffled babbling of the brook underneath the snow. Finally, though, they reached the basin, spread out completely flat, with the forest's undulating spruce boughs closing in above—a still-narrow path led to an almost sizable clearing. And all around, an incessant bubbling murmur rang through the Kolinda forest; secret, subterranean streams broke the surface here and there.

In the middle of the clearing, with snowdrifts all around it, stood the retired forest rangers' refuge. Like some sort of box full of secrets, its doors and windows were all boarded up. Even its tile roof was covered with freshly cut logs fastened with clamps to discourage anyone from trying to get in or out. And yet there was still life inside: tangled wisps of pale smoke hovered above the cracks in the tile roof, deliberate cracks that in these parts functioned as chimneys. Indeed, those within heard their steps approaching.

"Who goes there?" came the dull, hollow words from between the walls, as if from within a sealed box. "Who is it, and what do you want?"

"It's only us," declared Colonel Coca Mavrodin in her lusterless voice.

"Thank goodness. I recognize your voice, Miss. So you all came, after all, to let us out."

"Not quite yet. There's a little problem with your health, you know for a while longer. We can't be too careful. The weather's not too good, either—out here your colds would only get worse."

"It's good all the same that it's you people. Feels good to hear a familiar voice."

"Naturally it's us. And we brought you folks a little drink. I'm not even sure if it's a liqueur or rum. In a minute we'll figure out how to get it inside. We've got an iron Pope, so it would be best if we managed to pour it in through that."

"Liqueur or rum? Why, we thank you kindly in advance. Mr. Toni Waldhütter is here nudging me in the side, asking if the rum is Jamaican or Puerto Rican, because to him they're not the same sort of thing. I'm glad the old man has his voice back, though of course his question is just a joke."

"I understand, Mr. Toni Waldhütter—I too am picky about my drinks. Tell him he can taste it shortly. We've got Géza Hutira with us. He's a clever, resourceful man. No doubt he'll find a crack in the wall to stick the Pope in, and then in no time at all you can be drinking from the other end. It would be good if you hurry up and find a bowl to hold under the end of the Pope."

"Thank you kindly. We've been getting a bit low on provisions, too, in fact—enough for two days at most."

"Rest assured that you won't be needing any more—divide that up between you."

"Great—we'll get by."

At the edge of the clearing, just opposite the boarded-up house, were the three horses with their riders still mounted. Steam hovered all around them. Hoarfrost coated the riders' hair, and the men's beards and stubble. Even the yellow bits of cotton in Coca Mavrodin's ears had turned white.

"What's brewing here?" Géza Hutira whispered to Nikifor Tescovina.

"What do you think? Take a guess."

"Come on, really, what's up?"

"Leave me alone."

"Feel free to ask questions," Coca Mavrodin interrupted the two men. "I'll answer them. One of the retired forest rangers fell ill with the flu. And so now they're under quarantine."

"I didn't ask a thing, not a thing."

Géza Hutira spit on his palm: he must have understood that

he'd be the one to now give the retired forest rangers a drink. Getting off his horse, he removed the saddlebag containing two containers of rum from Coca Mavrodin's pommel; tied beside them he saw the long iron Pope she'd mentioned. He searched out the crack in the house the voices came through, slid the Pope in until he felt someone grab hold at the other end, then heard the Pope clink against the bowl they placed underneath. Slowly he began to pour. The rum, having congealed along the way from the cold, flowed sluggishly, like crystallized honey.

Meanwhile Coca Mavrodin, as if on a weekend outing, dismounted and took some snacks out of her coat pocket. She spread newspaper on the crusted snow, anchoring its four corners with chunks of ice to keep the wind from blowing it away. After tearing at the half-frozen potatoes with her nails, she asked Nikifor Tescovina for his pocketknife, with which she then sliced the onions. Next, as if yielding her portion to the men, she got back up on her saddle, bent her head down on the horse's neck, and seemed to doze off. Sunlight was fast fading from the clearing: twilight was approaching from the forest, and nighttime itself from the east.

"If by chance I also catch this illness," she grumbled, "you know what I'll do? I'll make my way through the barracks, spitting into the mouth of every single mountain infantryman."

"Probably not a bad idea," said Nikifor Tescovina, "but if you don't mind me saying so, I've heard that people who come down with the bug can't spit at all—even though their mouths are foaming."

"You still don't know me—I was just kidding. But where did you hear that about foaming mouths?"

"Doc, the bear warden. He said your mouth fills up with thick dry saliva—it's like a sponge, impossible to spit out."

Géza Hutira threw aside the now-empty containers and gazed after them, watching how easily they slid away over the snow.

Then he knelt down beside Nikifor Tescovina over the spread-out newspaper and the two began chowing down. Darkness was descending. The colorful light that had been streaming through the clouds now shone pale over the wind-swept snowdrifts.

"Hey, look," said Nikifor Tescovina when they had almost finished eating. "This onion ring here, why, it looks just like an ear."

"An ear? Stop kidding me."

"Take a closer look."

"Oh, it is an ear, a real ear, but how did it end up here?"

An entire ear lay among the cold potato skins and sliced onions and apples. A tad hairy, a tad bloody, clearly it had broken away—a fresh break—from somewhere or other not long before.

"If you don't mind my saying so," whispered Nikifor Tescovina, "you know, I think it is yours."

Géza Hutira clutched his head where his winter cap should have held down his ears. He groped about, then held out his palms before his face. One hand was still dry; the other, sticky, smudged, slightly brown.

"Hmm. Damn it. I must have hit something. I don't have a clue how this could have happened," he whimpered, as if making excuses. "Maybe it was that iron Pope, when I pulled it back out. It did knock against me a bit."

Coca Mavrodin was not asleep, after all. Sitting up straight in the steam wisps hovering about the horse's head, she cleared her throat and called out:

"Are you two kidding around, or is that really our comrade's ear? I'd like to take a look—let me see."

Géza Hutira had curled his palm around the hole where his ear had been so as to hear exactly what Coca Mavrodin wanted. He seemed to brood over what he'd just heard, and then, once he'd in fact understood, he sadly shook his head.

"Too late. . . ."

A four-legged little greenish-brown creature, the size of a

squirrel or a weasel, was just then scampering away over the crusty snow with the ear in its mouth. Its companion waited at a distance, and soon the crackle of Géza Hutira's cartilage could be heard as they crunched the ear between their teeth.

"I'll come up with something," said Coca Mavrodin much later on the way down from the Kolinda forest, "some sort of compensation. As far as I know, the Soviets are already making artificial ears. But if you'll excuse me for saying so, you might have been a bit more careful."

"No excuses necessary."

As before, they rode Indian file in each other's tracks, only this time they made a clearly visible groove on the *left* side of the road. The snow between the two trails remained untouched.

The stove was burning that night in Father Pantelimon's kitchen, and roasting on top were potato slices, mushroom caps, and whole unpeeled apples. The two colonels once again played nine-men's morris, though standing up this time, and with the door wide open. They kept playing, pushing the pieces across the tablecloth in silence, until the snowmobile once again buzzed in from beyond the snowdrifts. Now it pulled a sled loaded with rattling cans of gasoline and diesel oil. The driver might have been the same one who'd delivered the rum that morning, but it was impossible to tell: he had on a thick, glittery outfit; a copper helmet of the sort firemen wore; and boots that came right up to his knees. He didn't even get off.

"Can I get all the way out there with these?" he shouted over. His voice was as otherworldly as that of Géza Kökény. Coca Mavrodin and the priest went out to the verandah.

"All the way," replied Coca Mavrodin. "Just keep your eyes peeled. We left a groove of tracks on each side of the trail, so if you stick to the middle, following their shadows in the head-lights, you'll get there, no problem."

•

"Now I'd ask the two of you," Coca Mavrodin put in as she left in the morning once again on horseback with her men for the Kolinda forest, "not to piss along the way, no matter how much you have to go. Until I say now you can, hold it back. You're men, after all. It's not out of the question that we'll need a bit of warm fluid."

With his palm Géza Hutira formed a shell around the hole of his ear so as to hear what she was saying. Even so, Nikifor Tescovina had to explain what it was that Coca Mavrodin wanted.

They now proceeded between the two sets of hoofprints they'd made the previous day, on the snowmobile tracks, until they reached the point where only a narrow trail led the rest of the way to the clearing. There the horses came to a sudden halt, and no amount of goading could get them to continue. Only by getting off and pulling them by the reins could Coca Mavrodin and the two men drag the beasts to the final destination.

The place looked different than it had the day before. The snow was no longer white but gray, purple-blue, and in places completely black, and it was covered with hard blisters budding with purple lights and iron-gray flakes. And hovering in the frozen air was the smell of abandoned stoves and discarded flues. It was as if it had snowed ash all night long.

The boarded-up cabin where the retired forest rangers had once lived was gone. Undulating in the breeze, around a few obsolete, knotty black beams in the middle of the clearing, was a velvety mass of soot and ash. The snow after melting had frozen hard with ash flakes and glimmered everywhere like marble under the light of the passing clouds. A flock of birds, jackdaws, circled up high like a mass of trapped, swirling smoke from the conflagration. Scattered all about were discarded cans of gasoline and diesel oil.

After Coca Mavrodin wound a scarf around her neck up to

122

her chin, she got back on her horse, and started to trot about on the cinders: the horses now got to sneezing from all the stirred-up soot. Suddenly spurring her horse, she began to trample through the ruins. All the many clamps, clasps, and nails that had fallen out of the beams and the retired forest rangers' tools and sheet-metal pots now jingled under her horse's hooves. Colonel Coca Mavrodin then rode to the edge of the clearing and there stopped, waiting for her two men to follow.

"Come along now," she shouted, "There's nothing to worry about—the germs are all roasted away."

"What's she saying?" asked Géza Hutira, trying to catch Nikifor Tescovina's eye. But, sensing what he wanted, the other man looked away.

"Leave me out of this," warned Nikifor Tescovina, after a pause. "I don't have an opinion about any of it."

"I just thought you might have noticed what you've gotten mixed up in."

"What?! I don't know what you're talking about—we both work for Miss Coca, that's all I know."

Meanwhile, almost without realizing it, they too were trampling through the cinders at a slow trot and arriving at the far edge of the clearing. The horses kept snapping their feet up from the snow as if it were still hot.

"Let's have a bite," proposed Coca Mavrodin. "And today it's not just any old lunch. I brought a nice big jar full of carp with onions and crushed barley. And then, once you've had your fill, I'd like you to find the dog tags. I want three for each: like you they wore one on their necks, but they also had one on their wrists and their ankles. I'd appreciate your finding every last one."

Coca Mavrodin had carried the jar in her greatcoat pocket, but it wasn't necessary to unscrew the lid, because along the way the already congealed liquid had frozen, bursting the glass. Picking away the shards and slivers, she slowly freed the frozen cylinder of crushed barley and little dark blue fins. Next she broke it into pieces with her fingernails so they could be picked handily from her palms.

Lying all about on the crusty snow were various dead birds, their feathers charred black—crows, jackdaws, and thrushes. The fire must have awoken them, and no doubt they'd roasted in the air, but perhaps the heat had kept them afloat for a time, and then when the clearing below them cooled they'd plopped to the ground, scattered about.

As soon as they finished eating, Nikifor Tescovina got to work cutting spruce boughs and birch twigs while Géza Hutira broke off thick hazelnut branches. At first they poked around the whole site like treasure hunters, then, using clumps of twigs tied together with cords, they swept the ash from among the beams and the other remains.

"This is what they call black-market work," grumbled Géza Hutira. "Too bad I don't carry a mirror around—if only you could see how you look."

"Now what's your problem? My daughter seems to have had a really bad influence on you. Keep your clever little opinions to yourself."

With no ear on the side nearest Nikifor Tescovina, Géza Hutira barely heard what the other man had said. Twisting his head left and right, he looked about in confusion, probing the cinders.

In the end glazed thick with soot they found twelve sheet-metal dog tags dangling from chains. Coca Mavrodin then finally let them urinate. The warm, salty solution, she explained, would dissolve the soot, and then they'd only have to rub each tag in the crusty snow to read the engraved data.

Under the cinders and soot they'd found the dog tags of four men—which is to say, three dog tags each. But five retired forest rangers had lived in their forest retreat. Missing were the dog tags of one Aron Wargotzki.

•

Géza Hutira's lost ear meant that I was the one who later had to find Aron Wargotzki. On their way home, the three travelers once again took a break in my road worker's cabin, and Nikifor Tescovina and Géza Hutira were cleaned up: Elvira Spiridon soaked them with her watering can, while they, like tired horses in the rain, drooped their heads on each other's shoulders. Coca Mavrodin meanwhile called me out to the verandah for a consultation.

"Heaven took his ear, and I need a man with good hearing. And aside from him, no one knows the woods like you."

"That's not my territory," I said with hesitation in my voice. "You know perfectly well, Miss, that I've never set foot in the Kolinda forest in my life."

"But I'm now asking you, Andrei. Just this much, nothing more. Then I'll turn a blind eye to your business. Find this contagious individual for me—his name is Aron Wargotzki, remember that—and then I promise you that you can get out of here along with your adopted son."

From that day on, every morning I stood at the threshold, clamped on my cross-country skis, and then picked up my sweetheart, Elvira Spiridon, by putting one arm around her, and slid my way toward the Kolinda forest, dropping her off at home en route. Her husband, Severin Spiridon, was invariably waiting at the front gate. It was he who advised me to be especially alert on the tenth day; for that long a man can somehow scrape by in a dank lair of spruce cones sucking on saltless icicles, but then that's it: after ten days he'll crawl off on all fours to give himself up. And along the way his palms and knees will leave tracks in the snow.

For her part, this is what Coca Mavrodin said by way of farewell:

"You know what to really keep an eye out for, Andrei? Shit."

She wasn't talking nonsense. As all woodsmen know, even if a nighttime snowfall covers the shit Coca Mavrodin was thinking of, by morning, once the warmth of the sun soaks through its white blanket, its lying mask melts off and once again it gleams resplendently brown.

But Aron Wargotzki left behind no tracks—not of his feet, his palms, or his knees. Nor did I happen upon his droppings anywhere in the Kolinda forest. In the end, it wasn't ordinary human frailty that gave him away but instead his mindless desire for a life of luxury.

One afternoon before heading home—I was perhaps already into my second week of searching for him—I was taking a rest in the clearing once inhabited by the retired forest rangers, a clearing the snow had once again covered. While listening to the languid repetitive murmur of the subterranean stream as it rambled above the ground, the snow, the ice, and then back underneath, the unmistakable scent of scorched thyme hit my nose. This is what Géza Kökény smoked at the foot of his own bust, and this is what the bear wardens and sometimes the colonels themselves imbibed, too, when their tobacco ran out. On more than one occasion I'd tried it myself.

Just then the wind ceased for a few minutes, and blue tongues of smoke hovered in the blazing rays of sun shooting through the spruces and firs. In front of me in the snow, the elusive stream's path was marked by a shadowy depression, which ended in a gaping black cavity in the earth. It was from there, from time to time, that thin smoke went curling up into the air. While I'd been roaming the snowy woods in search of shit—following Coca Mavrodin's advice—Aron Wargotzki had been sitting there underground, smoking his Pope.

"Aron Wargotzki," I called out. "Give me your solemn promise not to move—I ask you sincerely to stay calm. You can't fly,

I hope, so wherever you might go, your tracks would give you away."

Aron Wargotzki kept smoking for quite a while yet. He replied only toward evening, when he'd determined that without a reply I would not budge an inch.

"All right, I promise. But only because I can't move—half my leg's burned off."

"Well, sit still, take care of yourself. And don't feel lonely, I'll be back soon—tomorrow morning at the latest."

I'd clamped my skis back on and had just about slid back across the clearing when his voice reached me yet again, resounding through the forest, booming along the deep and winding course of the subterranean stream.

"Géza, my friend, I want to ask you for a favor."

"You've got me confused with someone else. That's not me. But tell me what you want."

"If you know Géza Hutira, send him here. I've got to talk to him."

"I don't think he has any time right now, but if I run into him, what should I say?"

"That Aron Wargotzki asks him to come here. It's urgent—he should hurry up and bring along some warm milk."

"Alright—if I bump into him, and if I don't forget, I'll tell him."

"And who am I speaking to now?"

"Come on, Aron Wargotzki, you know full well I could say any old name to you—that's really not important."

My ski tracks had dug deeper into the snow each day, and so, concluding my business every evening, I set my skis in the grooves and slid right home to the pass, where Elvira Spiridon awaited me with a furrowed brow and gloomy eyes.

When I next appeared at the forest commissioner's office Coca Mavrodin was noticeably happier to see me. She showed me a rat trap with a very deadly spring: she'd been storing it in her desk drawer just waiting for the day I'd arrive with some news. She'd have five or six of them made—huge ones, of course—to be placed them at those points where the stream went underground to greet Aron Wargotzki in the event that he got better and tried to take off.

But Aron Wargotzki kept his promise. He did not move. Day by day the snow remained untouched where the stream went underground. Only a slender little forest mold–hued creature scurried past now and then—perhaps the same one that had eaten Géza Hutira's ear. Sometimes the scent of tart smoke wafted up out of the holes in the ground, and sometimes the odor of the spruce gum that had permeated this woodsman over the years.

"Listen, Aron Wargotzki," I called out. "I've spoken to Géza Hutira. He's a busy man—I'm afraid he just doesn't have the time to come up here. You'll have to settle for me. Tell me what's the matter, maybe I can help."

"Just talk him into coming by as soon as possible. I want to speak to him in private, that's all. And in the meantime, until he has the time, he should give you a jug of warm milk to bring out here for me."

"You're dreaming, Aron Wargotzki—what's this milk obsession of yours? Don't you realize you can't even swallow your own saliva? Your mouth is full of hard, dry foam. You're on your last leg."

"Me?"

"Yes—you're sick, I'm afraid. Very sick."

"Me? What are you saying? There's nothing wrong with me. It's just that I've eaten all this dirt and now I'd like a little milk to balance things out."

"Don't kid around, Aron Wargotzki. I know exactly what's wrong with you. That's why I'm asking you to sit tight: it's only for your own good."

"I've already said that I can't even move an inch, so where

am I supposed to go? The flesh burned off my right thigh—or, if you're looking at me, the left one—and what's missing is exactly that damn bit that used to move the leg."

"Well, just sit tight, and get through the next couple of days without milk."

While waiting for the traps to be finished, I spent each day in the clearing from early morning to sunset. The ski tracks led me straight to Aron Wargotzki. Sometimes I had to shout above the murmuring stream, calling out until he was finally willing to acknowledge that he had a visitor; and other times he was waiting right below the opening, panting with interest like a dog.

"Tell me," he pleaded. "What did my friend Géza say about me being here?"

"Nothing in particular, Aron Wargotzki. No one says anything about it. You know that's how things are."

"Well, when you bring the milk, be careful not to spill it and I'll tell you where to pour it in. I don't even care if you bring it in your mouth and spit it in some hole. As long as it's milk."

"Don't tell me you think I'd get that close—you really can't expect me to want to catch your flu."

"I already told you there's nothing wrong with me. It's just my leg that's bad ... and maybe I ate a bit too much dirt. It would be so good to rinse out my mouth with a little milk."

"Don't eat dirt—you'll get even sicker"

"And there's another thing that's bothering me. I'm sincerely sorry about Géza Hutira's ear. I don't even know how that happened, but I was so angry about that rum tasting nasty that I guess I shoved his iron Pope right back out. When I looked out, I could see at once that it broke the poor fellow's ear off, that it was hanging on only by a little flap of skin. I'd like to apologize to him. An ear isn't a small thing to lose."

"All right, I'll let him know you're sorry. He's a gracious, big-hearted man. He'll forgive you, Aron Wargotzki."

•

At the end of the day the mountain infantry's van was sup-posed to transport the traps to the road worker's cabin. Elvira Spiridon's hair, as well as the edge of her skirt, were fluttering in the twilight breeze. Beyond her, beside the fence and covered by a tarp to keep them from getting soaked in the event of a stray shower, were at least fifty bags of cement piled up in rows. Coca Mavrodin-Mahmudia had, it seemed, decided on another course of action.

"If you carry this out, sir," said Elvira Spiridon, leaning so close to me that I could smell the menace on her breath, "I would like it if we didn't meet while you do."

"All right—whatever you say. You're free—go, live your life."

In the week it took me to carry all those bags of cement on my back to the Kolinda forest, with several round trips each day, spring began. Pale grass followed by crocuses emerged on sun-soaked mounds of earth from under the blanket of melting snow, and the marble-white ski tracks etched two lines over the expanding patches of green. Misty blue thyme smoke hovered in the sunlight above the openings through which that subter-ranean stream breathed.

Once all the bags of cement were positioned by the open-ings, I threw a blade of grass on the water to see which way it flowed. I took out my freshly polished knife, and as I rolled up the sleeves of my jacket, the sunshine reflecting off the blade bounced into one dark lair after another: Aron Wargotzki ad-dressed me for the last time.

"You think I don't know what you're preparing? For that rea-son alone I'd like to know your name—for god's sake tell me who you are."

"Aron Wargotzki, I don't think this is the moment for intro-ductions, but the fact is I've been living in the Zone under the pseudonym Andrei Bodor. Please forgive the person who goes by such a name for this whole affair."

Coca Mavrodin-Mahmudia had not quite calculated right in ordering the bags of cement. Half were still untouched when the water turned gray, and slowed to a halt in the openings: the bubbles vanished from its surface; and, in a sign that as the solution was starting to bind and plugging up, all at once the stream sprung forth in several new spots on the clearing.

Standing where I'd left my skis at the clearning's edge was Elvira Spiridon in her new spring dress, fluttering in the wind; with her freshly washed, drying spring hair, and her enormous copper earrings glaring in the sun.

"So you're back, after all," I said, gasping for breath as I got near her.

"Today I began to miss you, sir."

There was no denying it: I'd missed her, too. As usual, I stood her on the skis in front of me, and as the forest began flitting by on both sides of us, gliding away backward ever faster toward the retired forest rangers' clearing, with my nails and my teeth I tore that new spring dress right off her, and, using my knife, I cut away at my cement-armored trousers until, finally, once again I felt her velvety behind on my lap.

11

SEVERIN SPIRIDON'S SURPRISE

The ramshackle little bus that made its way once a day over three mountain ranges between Sinistra and the Kolinda forest mainly transported the mountain infantrymen who patrolled the area, but also a few civilians who, with permits in their pockets, worked in one of the small high-altitude settlements. And when there were passengers, the bus stopped at the Baba Rotunda Pass, too, which was marked by a rust-eaten, paint-splotched iron post that would sway back and forth in the wind, its sign covered with drops of water left behind by a cloud tumbling through the pass and brushing the ground. Its creaking could be heard even through the closed window of the cabin where road worker Andrei Bodor lived.

One afternoon, well after the bus had passed by on its way from the Kolinda forest to Sinistra, a man came ambling across those snow-patched, crocus-dotted mountain meadows. His odd, sidling gait was reminiscent of a clumsy dog as he kept glancing left and right to avoid the black glitter of the snowmelt brooklets running haphazardly about. On reaching the road he paused, hesitating: he just leaned out over the paved surface, as if worried that its current would sweep him in one direction or the other. For a while he stood about, looking puzzled until he turned his head toward the creaking bus-stop sign. He then crouched down on the ground, planting himself at its foot: a wayfarer waiting for the bus.

He wore a black vinyl jacket, trousers glossy with grime, and a miner's helmet with a black visor. Hanging over his shoulder from a crooked walking stick was a black suitcase stuffed round. His skin was gray, his face shiny and hairless, with only a bit of sparse stubble around his chin. Oily eyes sparkled from shadowy, purple sockets.

The road worker, Andrei, kept a lookout from behind the window of his cabin, taking stock of the stranger through the 8 x 30 binoculars he'd gotten from Coca Mavrodin and that always hung on the doorknob. Through its lens the gray stranger was now wriggling about on the ground.

Occasionally he rose to stand beside the iron post, cupping his ears and peering out at the horizon suspiciously this way and that, and sometimes nervously jerking his head toward a passing flock of crows. He would also stare angrily at the late afternoon sun, whose languid yellow rays broke through narrow, leech-shaped clouds. From the corner of his eye he watched the road worker's cabin, too, as if aware that someone might be watching him from behind the window.

Someone was in fact watching him. Andrei had spent the previous night sitting up beside a dead bear warden—though he'd been officially relieved of his job as corpse watchman, he was often called upon to help out—and in the morning, when Colonel Titus Tomoioaga began his shift, the two of them had shared a little bottle of watered-down denatured alcohol. The colonel let Andrei in on the fact that a curfew was now in effect in Sinistra, and that maybe one would be announced here, in Dobrin City, as well. During the night someone had toppled the statue of Géza Kökény, so everyone would do well to stay home. Ever since the Sinistra puppeteers had held a dress re-hearsal on the streets and the mountain infantry had opened fire on them, patrols were roaming the village streets as well. Wherever you looked, long-necked young men, the gray gan-ders, were peering over fences into yards. Coal-scratched graffiti loomed on front gates and plank fences, slogans like "WE'RE WITH YOU!" or "THE LEAGUE IS WAITING FOR YOU TOO." With a heated iron bar, someone had burned into a wood fence: "PIGS."

It was toward the end of March, and the air was laden with disquieting scents; catkin pollen and flies were flitting about. At the bottom of the valley, the stream raged from all the snow-melt. Andrei had been on foot, halfway to the pass on the wind-ing mountain road, when the afternoon bus passed by coming from the opposite direction, from the Kolinda forest. All its win-dows were smashed in, and its passengers were not mountain infantrymen, but gray-skinned men in miner's helmets. A heavy, suffocating smell had lingered in their wake.

He was sipping at his first drink of the day in the road work-er's cabin when the stranger flashed before him at the far end of the clearing against the backdrop of the distant patches of snow. Before long his miner's helmet glimmered near the road as the man planted himself at the foot of the iron post. He kept turn-ing his head this way and that, but mostly toward that corner of the clearing beyond which, behind a cluster of spruces and firs, smoke was pouring from the chimney of Severin Spiridon's cabin. Then he refocused his attention on a stray dog crossing a nearby clearing—and once again he looked suspiciously at the road worker's cabin, behind the window of which Andrei, the road worker, was watching him. Every time the stranger looked up, his hard vinyl jacket crackled over his frame.

Time passed—the hopeless silence of twilight enveloped the clearings along with purple mists—and finally the stranger had

had enough of waiting. He stood up beside the iron post and headed up the slightly ascending trail toward the road worker's cabin. His helmet shimmered before him, reflecting sunlight that kept disappearing and then reappearing from behind a passing cloud. He went up the steps, and was just in the process of casting a shadow over his face with his palm, so as to peer through the window, when Andrei opened the door.

He looked exactly as he had in the binoculars: skin shiny and gray, unshaven but not bristly; he was the sort of fellow with just a sparse, hesitating film of stubble over his chin. His smell was staggering, as suffocating as a rural train-station waiting room—liquor, flea powder, and the kerosene used to mop the floors.

"What do you know about the bus?" he inquired quietly. "I mean, why doesn't it come?"

"It's already passed by," said the road worker.

"And the next one?"

"Only tomorrow afternoon."

Brushing against Andrei's chest, the stranger now stepped over the threshold and proceeded to walk once around the table in the middle of the cabin. He himself then closed the front door and turned the key in the lock from the inside. Letting it slip off the end of his hiking stick, his suitcase plopped to the floor with a heavy thud, as if packed full of rocks.

"Then I'm sleeping here," he said, unfastening his hard, cracked vinyl jacket; it crackled as he sat down at the table. Meanwhile his odor, like oil on water, spread through the cabin. As the jacket opened in front of his belly, it was apparent that his trousers were held up not by a belt but by a thick wire, which had a big loop where a buckle would have been, and lodged within that loop was a sharp-edged rock. He pulled a bottle from his inside jacket pocket.

"Want some?" he asked, glancing curtly at the road worker as he uncorked the bottle.

"Maybe later," said Andrei, declining the offer, pushing a mug over the table to the stranger.

But the other man drank straight from the bottle, sending bubbles racing the moment it touched his lips. After the first couple of gulps he removed his vinyl jacket and his helmet, placing them both on the table. His shiny gray scalp was matted with thin, sweaty strands of hair.

"Lie down for a rest now," said Andrei. "You can't stay here for long. I don't spend my nights alone, but with a woman."

"I said I'm staying here."

Andrei stuffed the stove with sawdust, spruce cones, and hard juniper roots, then lit a fire. He then went out to the verandah to bring in an armful of damp logs to dry out inside. By the time he returned, the stranger had moved from the table to the edge of the plank bed.

"Really no need to make a fire on account of me. My dad was an ice seller. We used to go out to the Kolinda forest to saw blocks of ice in the ice caves. The old man used to wrap them up in hay and carry them on his own back to the market for the rich people. Our family doesn't get chilled easily."

"This is the first time I've heard of the Kolinda ice caves."

"You'll never hear about them again, either. From what I hear, all sorts of people started to use them as hiding places, so they sealed them shut. With cement."

He stretched out his legs under the table and rolled up the sleeves of his grass-green sweater and the shirt underneath. His arms, laced with blue veins, were hairless and gray. Above a thin sinewy neck was a blunt chin. His eyes were oily, like elderberries.

"Are your papers in order?" asked the road worker.

"Mine?"

"This is a border zone, in case you didn't know, They keep government bears nearby."

"My papers? Yes indeed, mark my words. In perfect order.

Mine, of all papers! You can rest assured about them—"

"Okay, well then get yourself some rest. If you leave in the middle of the night, by morning you can catch the early morning train in Dobrin."

"That's what I figured, too."

The road worker took the binoculars off the door knob and then scanned the snowmelt-soaked meadows visible from the window. Night was coming, and dusk, which had already consumed the forest, now began enveloping everything at its edge. This was when Elvira Spiridon usually left home.

"Can I take a look, too?"

"Sure, go ahead. But you won't see anything worth looking at."

"I just want to see what you do."

"Here, take a peek. And tell me, if it's not a big secret: which way are you headed?"

After scanning the meadows, the stranger raised the binoculars higher to take in the ranges, and finally to the single cloud, which was glimmering like mother-of-pearl above the ridge in the light of the moon.

"Which way? I've got to be in Sinistra by morning, at the market. Something will be happening there."

"I've never seen you around here, you know."

"You've never seen me? No, you've never seen me. I'm not, you *see*—to use your words—from around here. My father and I would dare to go only as far as the Kolinda forest to saw blocks of ice. Earlier, as you know, that's where the border was. I don't know my way around here. I wanted to take a shortcut but lost my way. And meanwhile that damn bus went by."

Night was falling; Elvira Spiridon had set off from home. Although the stranger still held the binoculars, the woman's path could be made out from the birds taking flight before her. When her sloshing steps could be heard in the mud, Andrei went down to the road to get her.

"There's a man here," he said.

"The one with the black bag?"

"Yes."

Elvira Spiridon turned on her heels and headed back toward the house that was in fact her home. The road worker looked after her helplessly, staring with desire at the pleats of her skirt swaying back and forth over the curves of her behind. He kept his eye on her until she vanished amid a thicket of spruces and firs at a bend in the road. It was dark; every last cloud had disappeared from the sky; cold had descended into the pass; and between the rocks the mud began rustling as it hardened in the sudden freeze.

"I saw you send her away," said the stranger, breaking into a smile. "What a shame. Where's the poor thing going now?"

"To her husband."

The stranger's plum brandy was bitter. The steam surging from his nostrils as he gulped it down flashed hypnotically in the light of the fire. The road worker placed a tin plate in front of him along with a little water in a sheet-metal mug.

"If you get hungry, eat your cheese. I can smell it on you. You can get that sort of thing in your parts these days?"

"Oh, no. The only ones who got cheese got it on the road today. It would have been damn good to get to Sinistra by tonight. Like I said, something is happening there tomorrow."

"Get yourself some rest. Then make sure you're on your way before daybreak. Are you with the army?"

"With the army? I'll find that out tomorrow, too. The league will tell us who we're with."

The stranger presently loosened his trousers at the waist, and the sharp-edged rock fell from the loop to the floor and rolled away. The road worker got a pair of long-nose pliers, and while helping the stranger set the rock back into its mount, he noticed that the wire belt wrapped around the man's waist several times. The man sat patiently as Andrei tinkered at his belt.

"And what's it you do?"

"I work for the mountain infantry," said Andrei. "I'm in charge of this stretch of highway."

"Well, that's something! I thought it had to be this stretch of road. I figured you're an important fellow."

"Whatever you say, but you know, all the territory around here is off limits. It's all the mountain infantry's."

"Yeah, of course. Who's in command of the mountain infantry?"

"Coca Mavrodin."

"A woman? You're telling me it's a woman?"

"You got it."

"Well, it's not out of the question then that tomorrow, as soon as we take power, I'll have intercourse with her."

"Oh yes, when she sees you," said Andrei, taking stock of his guest, "she'll really want that, too."

The road worker now trimmed the wick on the hurricane lamp, lit it, and hung it on a long pole fixed to the gable of the cabin. They nearly had a falling out over this, for the stranger preferred that the cabin remain inconspicuous that night. But Andrei took the official list of road workers' rules and regulations off the wall and stuck it in the other man's face.

"All right already," said the stranger, rejecting the gesture with an open palm. "You don't seriously think I'm about to read all that, do you? Get it out of my face. All I'm saying is that I don't want some drifter winding up here on account of that flickering light. I don't mean the lady, of course."

"Later on I might fetch her, but I'll wait till you're asleep. It would be nice after you've gone to find her warm backside near me. In the meantime you can stretch out on the bed."

"Forget it. Don't you dare leave this shack—get it through your head that there won't be any more coming and going around here."

"I usually stand on the porch to piss."

"I'll go with you. How do I know you wouldn't be bringing some shady character down on my neck. After all, I don't really know you."

From the window the stranger had watched the road worker hang the hurricane lamp from the gable, disappearing around the corner of the cabin but soon reappearing out front, having walked around it. The moon was already above the ridgeline, the mud had frozen, and the pitter-patter of the stray dog's paws could be heard from the clearing. When Andrei got back inside, the stranger happened to be browsing the wall calendar—an old, fly-stained calendar from many years before, left there with its curled yellow corners, from the days of the previous road worker, Zoltán Marmorstein.

"What is this all about?" asked the stranger. "What sorts of numbers are these?"

"These numbers just show the days of the year, that's all."

"Are you Hungarian?"

"Half."

"Hm. That's nothing."

The stranger now stretched out on the plank bed, with his feet still in rubber boots propped on the headboard. Even while lying on his back he seemed to drink comfortably enough; only his Adam's Apple kept jumping about wildly as the plum brandy in his bottle fizzled with thick bubbles. Slowly the fire waned, then died out, and the crackling of the flue as it cooled down lulled the stranger to sleep. His head nodded to the side, his mouth opened halfway, and drool began to flow, forming a narrow sparkling band to his shoulder. The league's man had fallen asleep.

In his briefcase the sharp-edged rocks stirred, all by themselves.

Andrei the road worker tiptoed out of the cabin, removed the hurricane lamp from the gable, and carefully, to avoid crackling the veil-thin coating of ice under his feet on the freshly frozen puddles, crossed the road. On the clearing opposite him the stray dog's silhouette tottered, its eyes sometimes flickering with the light of the hurricane lamp. For a while it trailed in the road worker's wake, but midway there it sensed Severin Spiridon's dog in the dark and, breaking into a lively pace, moved on ahead. By the time the road worker reached the gate, the two dogs were already silently chumming up. Severin Spiridon was crouching under the eaves, leaning up against the side of the cabin.

"You've crossed my mind several times," he said to Andrei. "I'd gladly spend the night in the road worker's cabin in your place. I couldn't even shut my eyes; I just kept thinking of you."

"The fellow is asleep."

"But like I'm saying, I could have gone down right away, from the start—it just didn't occur to me at first. I'm not afraid of these people. And besides, I'd do anything for you, you know."

"Thanks."

"If you want to stay here, I can still go down. I'm sure I'll get along with him. I think I know his sort. The league is forming tomorrow in Sinistra."

"Okay with me. Go ahead if you want. But be careful: his bag is full of sharp-edged rocks. He wears the sharpest of them on his belt, in place of the buckle, mounted in wire."

"Trust me. Like I said, I get along with people like him."

Severin Spiridon headed off as Andrei, standing on the steps, watched. Elvira Spiridon now emerged beside him in silence, their hips already touching, the steam mixing in front of their faces as they waited for the flashlight to fade away at the end of the rimy meadow.

"Have you already slept with him?" asked Andrei.

"Only a little, sir."

"We should have a drink."

They drank blackberry wine, with its mousy aftertaste, ladling it from a wide-mouthed pickle jar into small mugs. A labyrinthine, branching metal object glinted at times against the sole source of light in the room, from the open door of the stove. It was a hair clipper, which lay alone on the middle of the tablecloth, its fine blades protruding menacingly like a row of tiny horns where the handles met. Andrei reached toward it, warily; it was cold, delicate. He looked it over thoroughly.

"What's this supposed to be?"

"My husband got it from the mountain infantrymen. The curfew is taking effect tomorrow. All the ones who must stay home have to cut off their hair."

"There was talk of hair-cutting back in the days of barber Vili Dunka. But then it didn't happen for some reason."

"This time we're supposed to do it ourselves. In fact I wanted to tell you, sir: tomorrow night, when I show up at your bedside, my hair will be gone."

The road worker kept dipping his mug into the pickle jar and taking gulps of the blackberry wine. Elvira Spiridon meanwhile slipped under the blanket, naked, leaving just enough room beside her for the man.

When not drinking, Andrei was busy stuffing roots into the wood stove and tossing in lots of spruce cones, which burned with a strong, white light. He then reached for the clipper and sat down in the chair beside the plank bed.

"I've never cut my own hair in my life," he whispered. "On the way here, I never thought today would be the day."

Putting one arm around Elvira Spiridon's shoulder, he positioned the clipper on the middle of his forehead, and began snipping, going on over the top of his head and down to the nape of his neck, then back again. As he might have done with some freshly ironed silk ties, he placed the fallen locks in a row over the back of the chair. Once he'd finished, and when the woman's bare head also shone, he dipped his mug into the pickle jar one more time.

But he took only a short break: no sooner had he emptied his mug than he folded back the blanket over Elvira Spiridon and placed the clipper on her belly, under her navel. With slow, tiny snips he proceeded downward, where a thick pelt of hair loomed darkly.

"They would have let us know, sir, if we also had to do it down there."

"This is my first time trying this," whispered the road worker, "so please, don't move."

She tensed up briefly, but as soon as the clippers grew warm against her skin, Elvira Spiridon relaxed, opening up so Andrei could access every single bit of her, every little mat of fur. Finally he took her in his lap, puckered his lips, and attentively blew his way over her body until not a strand of hair or fur was left.

"If I leave this place one day," he whispered into her ear in the middle of the night, "maybe I'll ask Severin Spiridon if he'll let me take you. If I were to decide to take you along."

"Give it a try, sir," Elvira Spiridon whispered back. "My husband would no doubt let you have me."

"I know I am talking about leaving this place—lately these thoughts are going through my head, but I hope you'll kindly keep this to yourself."

"Keep it to myself? Don't ask me such a thing, sir."

In the morning Elvira Spiridon tied a kerchief around her head, a kerchief she'd stuffed full of all the shorn locks of hair. The road worker meanwhile went about cutting fresh firewood to set by the stove, so Severin Spiridon would have yet another surprise. As he chopped up the old spruce logs, fat grubs plopped from the peeling bark to the gray, frozen ground, and even as he was swinging his axe and wood shavings were flying all about, massive crows swooped down to pick the grubs away.

"Isn't your belly cold?" asked the road worker as they walked in each other's steps toward his cabin. "Tell me the truth, please."

"I'm not exactly warm, sir."

"God knows what came over me. My nerves are shot. I had a really strange day yesterday."

"But sir, I think that even without hair you desire me."

"Oh yes, very much."

In the road worker's cabin Severin Spiridon was stretched out in his clothes, restlessly asleep, on the plank bed. The creaking of the floor as Andrei and Elvira Spiridon entered sent the bottle under the bed rolling to the middle of the room. In the center of the table, untouched and wrapped in newspaper, was a block of cheese left behind by the man of the League. As they peeled off the damp newsprint, they saw gray letters on the cheese. Severin Spiridon soon awoke, and recounted that by the time he had gotten there that night, the man of the League was gone. He'd left behind only that block of cheese and the bottle, which had in it just a little bitter plum brandy, but the entire cabin was permeated by the dreaded train station waiting room smell.

"Turn on the radio, please," said Severin Spiridon.

"Not now," the road worker replied.

"I'd like to know what's happening. The League is forming today in Sinistra. Please turn it on."

"I'm not the sort to listen to the radio. In any case, the radio can't be listened to just now—take a look for yourself: no batteries." The road worker showed him the broken, empty compartment in the back of the radio where someone had ripped out the batteries.

He now produced a little bottle of denatured alcohol, poured some into two mugs half-filled with water, then mixed in some spruce shavings he'd whittled with a knife, so as to allow the resin to soak in the bouquet.

"If you'll allow me," said Severin Spiridon around noon, "I'll take the woman along with me now."

Looking them over, Andrei first rested his eyes on Elvira Spiridon's matronly kerchief stuffed full of hair, then fixed them on her waist.

"Sure," he nodded.

"That man's smell has rattled me a bit, and I'd rather not be alone—let her spend the whole day with me, and at night I'll send her on her way, as usual."

"Take her. She's yours, after all."

Standing all alone for a bit at the window, which was buzzing with springtime flies, Andrei kept sipping at the liquor, staring out at the open areas beyond, and at the clouds passing by above them. Later, well into the afternoon, he took a walk on those spongy, snowmelt-sodden meadows. Not a soul stirred. About the couple of farms in the pass, only an orange-red fox tail flared up now and again behind the shriveling piles of snow by the woods, back among two purple heaps of ice.

He was on his way home again when a row of trucks, headlights beaming, approached on the steep winding road, making their way up toward the top of the pass. Each was covered by a canvas tarp. Cudgels, chains, and iron rods rattled in some of the trucks; others were packed full of slumped-over, dozing men. That suffocating scent of train station waiting rooms eddied in their wake.

Near the road worker's cabin, in one of the tire tracks, Andrei found an eyeball: solitary, coated with all the sticky grit and yellow fluid of mud, but an eyeball just the same—fallen, surely, from one of the canvas-covered trucks. Its oily shimmer was like one eye of that man of the League.

With the cabin still permeated by the stranger's smell, the road worker left the door open as he stepped in, and then opened the window. Until dusk he stood in the draft, leaning on the windowsill, puffing on his thyme-stuffed Pope. Then, carrying a bucket of water and a little camp shovel, he went down to the road, figuring that no matter whose it had been, he would bury that single eye. But he no longer found it there.

An orange-red double ribbon, a sunlit vapor trail, shimmied against the purple sky like the ski tracks the road worker had left on the clearings in the pass. Sitting in front of the open window, he waited; the scents of spring already hovered in the air, and even after dusk birdsong came in waves from the forest. Smoke soon rose straight up in the absence of a breeze from the wood-tile roof of Severin Spiridon's cabin, swathing the moon in a silvery light.

"From now on I'll wait for her in vain," Andrei Bodor, the road worker, thought to himself. "The curfew came into force today."

He was a bit annoyed at having been duped: his sly neighbor had secretly counted on that when taking his wife along home. And yet the road worker also imagined that the other man, too, would be in for a bit of a surprise when, kneeling in the sharp incandescence of glowing hot spruce cones, facing Elvira Spiridon's bare belly, he would face the naked truth.

12

NIKIFOR TESCOVINA'S CLOAK

When they found Petra Konnert, the railroad engineer's daughter, on the platform beside the night freight train, she was still alive, but it was her wish to be taken straight to the barracks' morgue. She'd traveled from Sinistra in a brakeman's cabin, and the moment the train had stopped she'd tumbled out and never moved again, except for the dark fluids flowing out from underneath her in all directions. Her father, Peter Konnert, lifted her like a sack of wheat into a creaky wheelbarrow and rolled her through the dark village in the middle of the night.

Work piled up in the morgue in early spring, and the mountain infantrymen often called in the road worker, Andrei, for auxiliary duty, which he invariably accepted in exchange for a bottle of denatured alcohol; and so he was the one who now helped lay the girl out on the grimy, gray stone table. By dawn the last signs of life passed out of Petra Konnert through so many wounds caused by arrows, spears, bullets. Disturbances had erupted the previous day in Sinistra, and puppeteers and jesters, brandishing theater props, had engaged in quite a bout.

As usual, Andrei opened the room's air vents, but on this morning, instead of dew-borne fragrances, an ignominious stink flooded in. On other spring days, the valley air was filled with the intoxicating scent of daphnes, those evergreen shrubs that bloomed during the night, but what now seeped through the vents into the morgue was the smell of human shit—the shit of the locals, and of the mountain infantrymen, still permeated by the musty bouquet of denatured alcohol.

No sooner had the sun risen and the fog lifted from the yard around the barracks than the explanation itself stank in full view on all sides. Daubed in a viscous brown glaze on the fences and walls—even on the wall of the morgue—was "YOUR MOTH-ER'S CUNT." It seemed one or two of the agitators of Sinistra had found their way to Dobrin.

When Andrei's night shift was over, Colonel Coca Mavrodin came to get him. That afternoon in the conservation area they were to distribute dog tags—the sort that were fastened to ankles and wrists. The jeep was waiting by the porter's booth at the barracks' front gate; on the back seat was a hemp sack full of the engraved, sheet-metal tags. The moment they turned out onto the road, a great big patch of snow shone before them, spread all over with huge brown letters: "UP YOUR MOTHER'S CUNT."

"This is the work of Géza Kökény," said Coca Mavrodin-Mahmudia. "I recognize the handwriting. If I only knew where he got all that shit."

Spring was in the air, and the snowmelt had turned the stream into a raging torrent full of wide cascades, with wagtails chirping away on its sparkling, foaming rocks. On the banks, lurking in the grass like secretive candles, were the purple flames of the dwarf gentians that had suddenly blossomed overnight.

"I have to admit I'm exhausted, Andrei."

"It's not good to share private matters with someone like me."

"Oh, that just slipped out."

Whenever a jeep wound its way that far up, its noise resounded all at once between the valley walls. Hardly would it have passed Colonel Jean Tomoioaga's sentry box by the crossing gate than already everyone above that point knew that the mountain infantry was on the way. By the time the jeep rounded the last bend in the road, Nikifor Tescovina would invariably be outside, standing between the oily puddles on the road.

Now, though, only a few crows bounced about amid the puddles, and no bluish curls of smoke hovered in the air above the wood shingles of the commissary. The door swung gently on its own now and again, touched by the breeze.

His back to the entrance, Nikifor Tescovina was rummaging about, stooped over a heap of satchels. He must surely have heard the jeep approaching along the steep road, its tires squelching in the mud. He must also have heard Coca Mavrodin's steps as she arrived on the threshold. But he did not turn around. His two little girls, their long black hair wrapped in kerchiefs, were sitting on the edge of the plank bed, pressed tight against each other. They wore white felt hats and brand-new knee-high moccasins fashioned out of rubber tires, as if dressed for the grandest of holidays.

"Are you traveling?" asked Coca Mavrodin, stepping around the bags.

"Me?" replied Nikifor Tescovina, standing up only after tying shut one of the satchels.

"It's just that all these bags gave me that idea."

"Oh, no. Sometimes I like to rearrange my things."

"Should I put the tags on them all the same?" asked Andrei, placing the hemp sack full of dog tags on the table. "Or no sense in that anymore?"

"Go ahead, as far as I'm concerned."

The girls' feet were grimy and smelled a bit of fungus once the socks came off. As Andrei groped at their ankles and wrists, their arms trembled and pea-size crystalline tears formed in the corner of their eyes.

"This is the newest craze," said Coca Mavrodin, "to go away. You caught it too, I see."

"I'm just rearranging my things," repeated Nikifor Tescovina.

But Coca Mavrodin no longer heard him. She'd stepped out of the commissary and had passed the jeep, walking toward the trail that led to Géza Hutira's cabin. Having flung the sack full of rattling sheet-metal dog tags over his shoulder, Andrei followed along behind. Nikifor Tescovina waited for Coca Mavrodin to reach the first trees that blocked her view, then signaled to get Andrei's attention, whispering *"Psst!"*

"What is it?" Andrei called back.

Nikifor Tescovina waited silently for Andrei to come near him and then, seizing Andrei's jacket above the chest, pulled him up close.

"You once told me that you'd show your gratitude if I wrangled you a job. Now's the time. I beg you, please give me a twenty. One of those twenties, I mean. I know you have a few."

"I can't," said Andrei, shaking his head. "Not that, Nikifor Tescovina. Just don't ask me for that."

"I know exactly where you keep them; Gábriel Dunka told me. If I want, I could even go there right now and help myself. But I respect you, and so instead I'm asking you, personally. Give me one of those twenties."

"I'm sorry, Nikifor Tescovina, but no! Soon I'll need every red cent—I'll need money like mad."

"Don't think I'm asking you to let me have it for nothing," said Nikifor Tescovina, gripping Andrei's jacket above his chest. "I hope you know me that well. I'll give you one of the kids. One is enough for me. I'm begging you, choose one—either one—so I can leave with the other one."

"I'm too old for them. And, as I said, I need the money. I can't part with even one cent. No, Nikifor Tescovina, I've said the last word on the subject."

Sitting on the ground between a cluster of newly grown nettles and docks, with the wind humming over the discarded bottles all around her, Coca Mavrodin-Mahmudia was waiting for Andrei by the red spring. From that spot, one could see out to the end of the valley, to the sparkling roof of Géza Hutira's cabin. Coca Mavrodin was watching his house through binoculars. She now turned toward the road worker and asked:

"Did he want money?"

"He brought it up."

"Bad timing, huh? Now of all times, when you also need it so much. But I bet he hardly expected to get something for nothing."

"Something like that."

"Too bad you're too old for that sort of thing."

Not long before, a rain cloud had passed over the river basin, and now a glassy roe of freezing raindrops shone among the spongy clumps of grass. The cabin's stone wall shimmered with thawing gray spots. On the inside, the window was covered with steam, which a hand sometimes wiped off so a face could peek outside.

The plank bed stood under the window, and on it, stretched out under a ragged blanket, was Géza Hutira. He held Bebe Tescovina with one arm, his beard mingling with the little girl's hair. The light of the snow-covered mountainside fell on their listless faces through the now open door.

"You've never come this way before," said Géza Hutira to Coca Mavrodin. "Something must have happened."

"I'm only curious to know the weather forecast. What do the instruments say?"

"I haven't had the time to take readings lately. Desire has had me in its fiendish grip."

"I only see now that we're the same age," Andrei Bodor interrupted as he pinched Géza Hutira's dog tag for a closer look. "We were both born in thirty-six."

"Don't let him tie those on us," Bebe Tescovina now said. "Please don't say another word to them."

"Yes, '36," grumbled Géza Hutira, "that was a very good year. We all made something of ourselves." He stroked, then ran his fingers through, Bebe Tescovina's short red hair. "Let him tie it on you if that's what he wants. Once they leave, we'll take them off."

The only sheet-metal dog tags left on the table were Béla Bundasian's. As if the three tags bore different names, Coca Mavrodin held each one up to the light and read them one by one before flicking each one out the open door onto the icy grass, the stones. She removed her cap. Then, who knows why, she rolled up the sleeves of her greatcoat just a bit and began climbing the ladder to the attic until her head reached the ceiling.

"I'd like for you to finally introduce me to your stepson, Andrei. I hope we find him at home."

With one hand she pressed open the trap door, and through the opening she peered into the darkness of the attic, which was broken only by the blades of light flashing through the cracks in the roof's wooden shingles. Béla Bundasian's eyeglasses sparkled among them.

"Allow me," said Andrei, standing on the ladder behind Coca Mavrodin, "to introduce Béla Bundasian, my stepson."

"Pleased to meet you, Bundasian. I've got to start with a confession—the Devil knows what came over me, but a moment ago I threw your dog tags out the door. They're not needed anymore. I came by to let you know."

"What are you saying?"

"I've erased you from the records. From what I know, your father has an acquaintance who will take the two of you far from here. You're strangers, so leave this place."

"I don't know you. How can I know what you want?"

"I promise—get out while you still can."

"At the moment, leaving is out of the question."

"Don't start making a fuss."

"Even you know I killed someone. I can't leave this place."

"Killed? Of course you haven't. You're mistaken, Bundasian; everyone is alive and well around you." On noticing that Béla Bundasian had dug his hands into the hay mattress and was now pressing some straw against his ears, as if he didn't want to hear another word, she added, "I'll send bats and owls here to squeak and hoot into your ears until you think it's over. If I've let you go, then—go."

By the time they climbed back down to leave the cabin, Géza Hutira and Bebe Tescovina were not to be seen. Only laughter bubbled out of the holes in the lovers' blanket, along with the jingling of the dog tags on their intertwined ankles and arms.

"What will you get by on when you leave?" Coca Mavrodin asked as she and Andrei walked back down. "How will you earn your living?"

"I've been thinking of bone carving, Miss."

"What am I supposed to make of that?"

"While wandering about the woods I've found lots of bones, and I've been giving carving a try: flowers, deer, mushrooms, colonels standing watch. People go for that sort of thing."

Every single window of the commissary was smashed, and birds fluttered in the empty room inside. Moss had already encroached over the threshold, and the door suddenly creaked with age in the wind. On it hung Nikifor Tescovina's cloak, which he'd tied with wire, piece by piece, out of Gábriel Dunka's marmots. It even had a hood, and from it hung a piece of birch bark scribbled with these words: *"I'm taking a twenty after all, Andrei. You'll need this cloak of mine, otherwise you'll freeze among all that cold mutton."*

13

GABRIEL DUNKA'S NAME DAY

At the age of thirty-seven, Gábriel Dunka saw a naked woman for the first time in his life. True, he was a dwarf. He was on his way home in his red van from the building site of the new Sinistra prison when Elvira Spiridon flagged him down. Sleet had been falling since early morning and a dank fog enveloped the spruces and black alders along the stream, and wind-whipped wisps of it were drifting over the road. The drenched form of the woman stood glimmering within them like a porcelain figurine. She was completely nude but for her thick head of hair, matted against her neck like an old, threadbare scarf. Her wet thighs, her loins strewn with spruce needles and with blue, white, and yellow flower petals had seemingly blossomed in the spring storm.

Gábriel Dunka recognized the woman, who lived in the Baba Rotunda Pass and sometimes passed along the fence of his house on her way to the fruit depot with a mushroom-filled satchel or a pack basket full of blueberries or blackberries. Never would he have thought that one day, stark naked at the side of the road, she would flag him down—him, of all people. Reluctantly, he picked her up.

Rather than have her sit next to him up front, concerned that someone might see her there instead he had her lie down in the back among the wood frames he used to keep window panes apart while being transported. The station wagon was not actually his own. He used it only to drive the glass between his workshop in Dobrin City and the construction site in Sinistra; the prison directorate and the mountain infantry commander drove those roads by special permit. Explaining himself would have been a challenge, were some official or even a local peasant to notice that he was now, while on duty in his yellow-plated official car, transporting nude women. Having stretched out Elvira Spiridon beside the frames, Gábriel Dunka slammed the rear door shut.

Gábriel Dunka was only as tall as the woman's belly, and having breathed in the intermingled scent of her navel and the rain on her skin, he was now a bit dizzy.

As soon as he got home—the shed, set in a simple, bare village yard, was also his workshop—he backed in right up to his door so as to get the woman inside without attracting attention. The neighbors across the stream watched his every move through binoculars, he knew—for many people could never get their fill of the spectacle of a dwarf.

As might be imagined, Elvira Spiridon hadn't exactly been engaging in innocent pastimes. That morning she had tried to flee the country along with her companion, but the attempt turned out badly for her from the start.

Mustafa Mukkerman, the Turkish trucker, transported frozen mutton from the Beskids range to the southern tip of the Balkans and sometimes, on the side, he smuggled out desperate people by stashing them among the halves of icy sheep, which hung on hooks. On this day he had left her behind. It turned out—as they discovered only just as they were clambering up—

that he had long before sworn to himself never to transport women; some nervous wench had once messed up the whole truck. So while her companion, Andrei, the road worker, was put aboard, she, Elvira Spiridon, had to stay behind on the road, and stark naked at that.

It had been raining that day since the wee hours, so Andrei Bodor and Elvira Spiridon had undressed completely; climbing into the dark rimy frozen compartment while sopping wet would have meant death itself. They'd stuffed their clothes into a single plastic bag brought along for that purpose, figuring they would get dressed again once they were on their way, safe inside. For a while the woman wrangled with the driver, but in vain. By the time reality sank in, the truck—with both Andrei and the packed clothes inside—was on its way again, on its way south, to the southern Balkans, where the lights of freedom glitter night and day. Elvira Spiridon stayed behind, naked, in the thick gray fog.

For a while she sobbed, then she pulled herself together enough to pluck an ivy leaf off a nearby bush to cover her lower belly. She must have seen this sort of thing in an old photo. But the wind soon tore the leaf away.

Elvira Spiridon wandered about half the morning amid spruces, denuded birches, and black alders until finally the dwarf glass worker's station wagon emerged from the heart of the fog, its official yellow license plate shining. There was no mistaking it: aside from the vehicles operated by the mountain infantry, which were recognizable from afar on account of their sputtering old engines, this more or less civilian-looking red motor vehicle was the only one that regularly traversed the whole of this mountain region.

Notwithstanding his unusual size, Gábriel Dunka was a state worker, an artisan. In those days his job was to frost the windows of the Sinistra prison, which was then under construction.

Every time he finished a batch—thirty-five or forty windows a week—he himself loaded up his station wagon and set out for the site. In the middle of his shed was a huge crate full of sand, with a plate of smooth glass under the sand. The dwarf moved about in his bare feet inside that crate scratching up the glass until it was no longer transparent.

The sand was piled up beside the crate, too, and that is where Gábriel Dunka set Elvira Spiridon.

"I ask for your patience," he said in a hushed, awkward voice. "In a moment I'll find you one or two pieces of clothing that should do."

He now picked up the brown paper bag he'd been using as a rug, tore it halfway open, and used it to cover the naked woman. Rainwater, still seeping from Elvira Spiridon's every crevice and orifice, ran in all directions onto the sand beneath her.

"You're really a very interesting man," said Elvira Spiridon, "to give someone a helping hand when they're in trouble."

"Trouble is right," replied the dwarf. "Which is why I'll ask you not to move too much. Just lie down there for the time being if possible. I can't be seen in the window, or my neighbors, if they notice any movement, would know there's a stranger here."

Having stuffed the iron stove full of sawdust and spruce cones, Gábriel Dunka lit the fire. Once the heap of tinder and kindling was blazing, he threw on a fair-sized barrel stave as well. Not long before, the nearby wild fruit depot had been shut down, and old barrels left there were quickly taken apart and distributed for use as firewood. The crackling stave emitted bluish-green tongues of flame with a heady scent of fruit. Elvira Spiridon shivered under the torn paper bag.

"I myself would have been dry by now," observed Gábriel Dunka in a somewhat embarrassed tone, aiming in part to lighten the mood. "Since I'm smaller. Naturally, if something is smaller, for example a dwarf, it dries faster."

"I've already learned something new," came Elvira Spiridon's voice from under the paper bag. "But you know, maybe it's a little strict to call yourself a dwarf."

Gábriel Dunka kept his every possession in a threadbare old vulcanized-fiber trunk that served as a shelf between his bed and the shed's clammy wall. He now opened this and rummaged about, up to his elbows in the heap of gray and yellow stained, bug-spotted, mouse-scented clothes. He picked out a few pieces and put them aside.

"Are there batteries in your radio?" Elvira Spiridon suddenly asked. "Maybe they'll have something to announce."

"There are batteries—but I'd like to be able to hear if someone is coming this way through the yard. It's possible my neighbors may have gotten suspicious, after all."

"I'm not scared here with you. No matter what happens, I'm sure you'll figure something out. Don't be offended by my saying so, but looking at you, I see a man from head to toe."

"Thanks. But you know, occassionallly one or two colonels stop by, curious to know how I frost the window panes."

"Oh dear."

"But not too often. All the same, if any visitors turn up, not a single part of you should be showing. And no loud breathing, either."

Taking in his arms the heap of clothes he'd picked out, Gábriel Dunka plopped them down in front of Elvira Spiridon. Lifting the torn paper bag off, he now saw to the task of dressing her. First he tried a pair of shorts with suspenders, but for all his efforts, he couldn't pull them up even as far as her knees.

"I figured they might not be good, But I wanted to see how they look. But forgive me, I feel really strange. Because I touched your skin, I guess.... It's lovely, but I'm a bit dizzy. I feel I can't quite breathe right now."

Backing away from the woman, Gábriel Dunka now leaned

over a water-filled bucket, first dipping his whole face inside, then lapping some up. He didn't dry himself off with a towel after, but instead just let the water run down his neck.

Elvira Spiridon began to dress herself, pulling one entire pair of pants up over one leg, then another over the next; and she then covered herself back and front with two jackets she tied together at the sleeves.

Gábriel Dunka had meanwhile busied himself, rattling pots and pans, and filling a pot with water and waiting by the stove for it to boil. He then mixed in dried blueberry leaves. After letting the concoction seep for a while, he poured it into two sheet-metal mugs. Once the tea looked done, he produced a one-liter bottle bearing an official blue seal and poured its contents—blue denatured alcohol— liberally into each mug. Finally he set one of the steaming mugs in the sand close to Elvira Spiridon.

"Cheers. Welcome. Heaven must have wanted this to happen."

"Cheers, Mr. Dunka. I think it's just about Gábriel Day now."

"Maybe so."

"I hope I won't be a burden."

"If you don't move, then I think you won't be much of one, and you can stay as long as you like. Or until I have to leave. Which might happen soon."

"I'd be truly sorry."

"Yes, it could in fact happen that one fine day I'll leave. Not to the far south, Elvira, but off to be among the residents at the Sinistra Museum. Not long ago I sold myself to them. I sold my skeleton to its natural history collection. I now belong to them. They like to collect such things, you know—and they paid me in advance."

"Yes, I've heard that the museum is full of all sorts of interesting things."

"That's a fact. And I'm sure they want to see their investments pay off. Will they wait for me to turn up my toes? Who knows—

maybe one fine day they'll come to get me. How's the tea?"

"I was just about to say it's delicious."

"Maybe we'd better now keep quiet. Even the glass has ears."

Night was falling fast outside, the shed's tiny windows taking on a bluish tint. Once it was dark enough that the reflection of his face began to show on the glass, Gábriel Dunka set a branch alight and used the flame to light a candle. Next he shaved, then rubbed half a handful of crushed thyme over his moist skin. He donned an old yellowish shirt, soft from so much washing, along with the jacket of his onetime school uniform, which had been lying wrinkled at the bottom of the trunk for years. The day had come to put it on again.

"I'm sure you notice," he whispered, "that I'm a bit nervous. Tonight I'll be with a woman for the first time. Why, look— even the hair on the top of my head is trembling."

"There's no need to be nervous," replied Elvira Spiridon. "It's not as if it's any big secret to-do—you must have heard what it's all about."

"I'm ashamed to say I'm a complete novice. But dwarves do have a rather good reputation."

"That's exactly why you should relax and also just remember, too, what an awful fix I'm in."

Gábriel Dunka shuddered; he gave a big sigh. Without a doubt, the woman's skin—or, rather, the disquieting whiteness which had shone from under the brown paper bag—was different than it had seemed at first sight, when, bedraggled, she'd stood before him out on the highway, her shoulders purple with fear, her nose a deathly white, her earlobes drained of blood.

"Please don't take me for a boor," he said in a hushed but agitated tone: "I've got to leave you on your own for a bit. I'll return once I've calmed down. I don't know what's come over me, but I've got to go, I feel so awfully strange. I'm afraid I might even kill myself."

"Of course, Mr. Dunka, go ahead. Take a little break. If don't mind, I'll fill my glass now and again while you're out. By the time you get home I'll be all warmed up."

For years now there had been no street lamps on the main road through Dobrin City, which followed the course of the stream, through the bottom of the valley, and took a curve up toward the pass. People around there, if they chanced to cross paths in the night, recognized each other by their smells. Doddering along among puddles that glimmered in the distant light, Gábriel Dunka might have seemed, from afar, like a dog. Only his steps squelched differently in the mud.

He walked out of the village to the crossing gate and the guard booth at the entrance to the conservation area entrance. Gábriel Dunka was in the habit of dropping by to visit Colonel Jean Tomoioaga, who for years had manned this post alone and lived in the booth. Whenever the dwarf showed up, the colonel would spread his green-and-white checkered shirt on the floor, take out the chess pieces he'd carved himself along with some pebbles of various unusual colors, and they would play a few games.

And that's what happened that evening, too. But Gábriel Dunka quickly became visibly tired of playing. Indeed, Colonel Jean Tomoioaga, noticing that his mind was elsewhere, discreetly pointed out his mistakes. Even so, that night the dwarf lost every single game.

"There's no point in playing," Colonel Jean Tomoioaga finally declared. "I'll just keep thrashing you. What's eating you?"

"I hope you're sincerely interested—I can't keep it to myself. That's why I stopped by so late at night: I need to file a report."

"You're an insider—you can do it yourself."

"I should go to Sinistra right away with the information, but after sunset I'm not allowed to use the car. It's a serious matter: an illegal border crossing."

"All right, I'll take care of it in the morning."

"Not in the morning—now. The individual must really have been up to some mischief, she didn't have any clothes on. She can be found at my workshop. Do something—have her taken away immediately."

The last person to see Elvira Spiridon in Dobrin was Géza Kökény. It was not a joyous occasion. As if still worried about the neighbors watching, the woman crawled out of the dwarf's workshop on all fours, her beautiful belly arcing toward the ground as she crawled toward the jeep waiting by the bust.

Before long, Gábriel Dunka got home, where he was greeted once again by the cold silence of the window panes. The scent of soaked skin, hair, and secret crevices escaped the moment he opened the door, swept away forever by the Sinistra winds.

14

BÉLA BUNDASIAN'S FIRE

On the last day of his life, Béla Bundasian awoke to find himself all alone in Géza Hutira's cabin. Freezing rain had been pattering all night against the wood shingle roof, and in the early morning, when it suddenly stopped, a bleak silence went on hissing in the empty room, the quivering ash droning inside the stove. But then the flue resounded with a hooting noise: the owls Coca Mavrodin had promised had no doubt arrived.

Descending from the attic, he saw that the cottage had been abandoned. Missing were Géza Hutira's rubberized, hooded windbreaker, which at other times would have been hanging from the doorknob; his bag; his binoculars; and even his crampons. The hay on the empty plank bed still bore the impression of Bebe Tescovina's curled up frame, and hovering in the air above it, it seemed, was the odor of nascent milk. But the happy couple was far away by now.

Outside, everything—every piece of wood, every stone, each of the few steps up to the cabin—was sheathed by the drizzle's icy glaze. Pressing his hands against the cabin's exterior stone wall to keep from slipping, Béla Bundasian managed to walk its length, then a few more steps over the ice to the nearby shed.

There he rummaged about for screws, which he drilled into the soles of his hiking boots so he, too, could get on the road all the sooner. Once the freezing rain had passed, the peaks and mountain slopes opposite sparkled with a diamond-like light, as if liquid glass had poured all over them, and all around the cabin, blades of grass tinkled in the wind like cups clinking against each other.

From deep in the forest down in the valley came a metallic scratching, the jingling of crampons. But it was only an echo: by then Géza Hutira and Bebe Tescovina were already traversing the precipices along the top of the ridge.

Donning his glasses, Béla Bundasian soon caught a glimpse of them on high. At first the two appeared to be a single, point-like object that kept appearing and disappearing among the crags, but soon the rising sun projected the contours of the entire range onto a passing cloud of freezing rain, magnifying Géza Hutira's silhouette. With soaring steps he swished above the ridge, carrying Bebe Tescovina on his shoulders, his head bent forward to keep from pressing against the child's belly. Clouds carried them off toward the Ukraine.

Béla Bundasian filled the pocket of his jacket with dried mushrooms, dried cranberries, and beechnuts. With a pick-axe he then smashed in the door, bashed in the window and the roof shingles, and even managed to ravage the stone wall with a few choice blows to the corner of the cabin—paving the way for the rains and winds to come. Hands clasped, he now kneeled in front of the ruins, but when the wind swept a piece of string before him, he snatched it up and tied his glasses around his neck to keep them from being lost, when knocked off by the branches that, he knew, would tear at his face as he bushwhacked his way down the slope.

Gripping onto rocks, branches, and clumps of grass, he made his way down into the valley. Behind him, the cabin's now ex-posed beams were already occupied by crows.

Further down, an ungainly mass of ice loomed near the bubbling spring. Frozen inside was a glittering red star from a gray
mountain infantry cape's collar.

At the commissary, birds whooshed about among the cabin's
broken windows and the threshold, as if now furnished with a
welcome mat, was moss-covered, with two yawning marmots
on top.

In the guard booth, lying on his back and snoring on the plank
bed, was Colonel Jean Tomoioaga.

"Don't take my waking you up the wrong way," Béla Bundasian whispered into his ear, "but I've noticed that everyone
is taking off while I stay behind scot free. Please put me under
arrest."

"I can't. Don't even ask—you've been erased from the records—as far as we're concerned you no longer exist. Get out
of here, leave."

"For god's sake you could at least try. You got rid of Elvira
Spiridon—and I killed someone, after all."

"Whether you killed someone or not, that's your business. I
suggest you steer clear of Dobrin: no one around here knows
you anymore."

Willow catkin pollen hovered in the air above the Sinistra
River along with the sound of thrushes singing and the heady
fragrance of daphnes.

Once he was near the village, Béla Bundasian veered off the
road, went around a boggy meadow full of dwarf birches and
black alders, and then went around Dobrin City itself, which
was for all intents and purposes off limits to him. At the far
end of the village, at the foot of Pop Ivan Mountain, he finally
reached the north-south highway. Glaring in one fold of the
slope were the blue and yellow walls of the gas station.

"What day is it today?" he asked on arriving at the station.

"Monday, Tuesday, something like that," replied Géza Kökény,
the attendant.

"So it's not Thursday."

"Not a chance. That much I know."

Béla Bundasian lay down for a rest, stretching out on his back for a little while in a roadside clearing. He stared up at the clouds, at the birds passing by above him, at the insects zigzagging about in the air. Then he sat up and watched the winding mountain road. Hours passed; not a single vehicle went by. He staggered to his feet, moved his numb limbs, stretched, and walked around the gas station.

"How about a round of nine-men's morris?" asked Géza Kökény.

"I just happen to have the time—if you agree not to cheat."

They drew the board on the oily ground and moved the pieces—stones and pieces of wood—around with their feet. No one disturbed them; no one pulled up to the station. In the afternoon, a solitary horse strode over the meadow across the highway on its way to a nearby watering hole. Its pale, badgery hue was like that of the snowmelt-soaked mountainside.

The two men followed this horse with their eyes: like some divine messenger, secret signals of light glimmered all along its mane as it ambled silently on.

"And if by chance it was Thursday, it still wouldn't do you any good. Mustafa Mukkerman isn't coming anymore. So there's no point in waiting around here."

"That makes things look different: maybe I should rethink my day."

"I couldn't keep silent about it. Here at the station you can get oil and gas, but unfortunately I can't help out with anything else."

On finishing the game, Béla Bundasian once again walked around the station, and again he stretched out on the roadside clearing, chewing on the seeds, the dried mushrooms, and the dried cranberries in his pocket. He dozed off a bit, too, amid the distant rumble of the mountain infantrymen's jeeps as they crossed from smooth, grassy ground onto the rough highway. Then, silence anew. He awoke with a start, patted down his empty pockets and the rest of his body, and staggered to his feet. He stretched, spit once or twice, farted, then ambled over to the gas station and woke up Géza Kökény.

"All right, then give me a can of gasoline and a container of oil."

He paid with the twenty dollar bill his stepfather had once given him. He got so much change in return—in coins in the local currency—that all his pockets were overflowing. Swinging the can of gasoline at his side, he crossed the road to the meadow, ambled along the tracks left by the badger-hued saintly horse, toward the far end, over by the old mill, the onetime fruit depot.

By now he felt to the bone that these were the final steps of his life, and a wild passion came over him: at first his ragged trousers showed only a bulge, but then his penis broke through the front buttons and sprung out into the air, pointing at the sky.

Béla Bundasian stopped at the bank of the stream, where the grove of willows obscured his view of the village; above the bloomy catkins slowly vanishing diamond peaks still shone. Freshly blossomed dark blue flowers—dwarf gentians—fluttered in the yellowish-green grass before his feet like burning candles. He removed his hiking boots, placed them carefully beside each other, and stuffed his toe-rags inside. Like before bedtime, he would have been happy to take a piss, but he quickly gave up on the idea: as a man he knew that that was a no-go just now, not with his member as stiff as a flagpole. There was nothing to be done about that. And so he listlessly picked a gentian flower and tried pinning it to the opening of his urethra. But it just popped back out, falling to his feet like a tiny blue candle—a candle whose flame, he imagined, would soon set him ablaze.

Even his fingernails glowed red hot; his ears and the tip of his nose threw off sparks; his pockets ripped out, sending all those coins bouncing about the ground, scorching the grass, smoldering the dirt. Even the frames of his glasses melted, but the heat kept the lenses hovering before his eyes for a good long while yet, and so before he went sprawling into the stream, to be swept away like flakes of lichen, he must have caught a glimpse of the curious onlookers assembled around him, their eyes reflecting the scene all with the glassy indifference that is a stranger's due, and no doubt he was almost sorry about the whole thing.

Years later I turned up once again in Dobrin, and there met Géza Kökény, too. He swore it wasn't the stream that had swept him away but, rather, the wind, which had carried him off bit by bit over the course of a week or two, sizzling and smoldering among the blossoming gentians like a wet log in a fire, and during that time the badger-hued horse avoided the meadow on the way to its watering hole.

15

GÉZA KÖKÉNY'S NIGHT

For years I had owed Gábriel Dunka four twenty dollar bills, and one day, intending to finally settle the debt, I set out to look him up in his old place. It was a spring afternoon when I arrived in the Baba Rotunda Pass in my brand new, metallic green, four-wheel-drive Suzuki jeep, a Greek passport in my pocket. After so many years, it was as if I were glimpsing the Sinistra river basin for the first time. At the far end of its kaleidoscope of colors and shadows stood the lofty peaks of Mount Dobrin, swathed by the glowing, turquoise hues of the nighttime horizon.

I thought I'd leave the jeep in front of the road worker's cabin—where I'd once lived myself for a couple of months—and walk around the summit, but I found neither the road worker's cabin nor Severin Spiridon's farm; their exact locations could only be guessed on the basis of a few dark blue rain-soaked heaps of cinder and ash. Nothing else had changed in the Baba Rotunda pass: a metal post glistened on a nearby ledge; a bat with ragged wings hovered above the western horizon; and an enormous, orange-red cloud hovered to the east. Even my old ski tracks still wound their way toward the Kolinda forest. The marble-hued double ribbon, winding over grass whose verdant green shimmered in the reflection of a passing cloud, went along past illuminated resin-splotched tree trunks and secret mountain meadow corners.

As was customary, in Dobrin I reported at once with the mountain infantrymen, who designated the newly built inn as the accommodation where I could pass the twenty-four hours allowed for my visit. The young colonel, still practically a child—her face caked with powder, her lips smeared with lipstick—warned me to occupy my room soon and not to leave it that day, since the curfew took effect at sunset, as it had every evening for years. Night was falling fast: beyond the springtime leaves, Géza Kökény's bust seemed to be submerging into the crimson light of the setting sun.

In the bar at the inn, floating in a little puddle of stinking grease in an open metal can, was a wick whose flickering flame lit up the scruffy face of the bartender—my onetime chum and chess partner, Colonel Jean Tomoioaga. He stood there in a tank top; in patched-up, stained army trousers; with long, pointy griffin-like toenails drooping floorward from the end of his leather sandals. The posh scent of cedar that no doubt hovered about me seemed to take him aback along with my silver hair—tied up in a knot just now with a dark blue ribbon of silk. From that point on, though, neither my face nor my voice seemed to interest him. Did he recognize me behind this pageantry of fragrances and colors? I could only guess.

Inquiring about a certain dwarf named Gábriel Dunka, I expressed my hope that I'd find him in good health at his old address. Although he had known him well—he had been another of his chess partners at one time, after all—the bartender Jean Tomoioaga now didn't even bat an eye.

"Dwarf? Can't say I know." He shrugged his shoulders, looked out the window. "Don't come looking for a dwarf here. Even if there had been one at one time, he's no longer here."

"Maybe he moved?"

"You might say so, sir. But that's enough already. If you wish to know more, inquire in person in Sinistra, at the museum's natural history collection."

He poured me a tiny dose of cheap rum—into a glass with a bit of tart gentian root at the bottom. Though the liquor stung my throat a bit, I was so partial to this sort of bouquet that I would gladly have downed one or even two full shot glasses. But the bartender Jean Tomoioaga rushed me away: "It wouldn't hurt if you now turned in, too, sir. In case you haven't noticed, folks around here have long gone to bed."

I kept staring out the window of my room at those lofty peaks until, finally, they were swallowed up by the purple darkness approaching from the east. But the moon was also taking shape behind Mount Dobrin, its coppery light flooding the sky around it. A furry, fluffy little cloud now settled on one of the ridges, its shape practically the same as that of the little creature which so long ago had eaten Géza Hutira's ear.

That brought to mind Géza Hutira, who, it was said, had not shaved in twenty-three years. He in turn brought to mind the sacked barber of Dobrin, Vili Dunka, who then brought to mind his onetime live-in lover, Aranka Westin—whom I'd parted from exactly seven years earlier without so much as a farewell. Perhaps it was not yet too late to make my excuses.

Stepping out of the window into the inn's yard, which was overgrown with nettles and docks, I passed into the darkness and through familiar yards toward my old girlfriend's house. My plan of a little joke—sneaking in on all fours and stretching out on the rag rug by her bed like a groveling dog—fell flat, however. Aranka Westin must have been on the alert, for all at once she swung open the door before me. Not that she could have seen me without electricity to turn on a light, nor could she have recognized me by my silhouette alone. At most,

I might have given myself away by the tart fragrance of spotted gentian, which on my breath that evening, as in the old days, was always one step ahead of me. She knew just who I was, addressing me by my old pseudonym.

"I knew you were alive somewhere, Andrei. And I also knew I'd cross your mind some day."

"I came by," said I, practically choking with emotion, "to apologize."

Out of propriety we exchanged small talk for a while, but in the darkness our hands, while undoing buttons and laces, met in ever barer places, until finally we'd shed every bit of clothing from our bodies. As if water were trickling from under her, her skin was cool; the bed of fur under her belly had long gone extinct; and our knuckles thumped against each other like juniper roots. What happened, happened, and never will I regret it.

Languidly, tapping at my artery, I lay there nestled close to her warmth when, all at once, wild geese honked from the clouds above us. They'd long settled on this homebound route toward Scandinavia. I swear there's not a sound more disquieting than theirs. As could be heard unmistakably through the silence of the night, they were coming from the south, from the Kolinda forest; and on arriving above Dobrin they'd turned suddenly north, toward Pop Ivan Mountain. Their calls stirred the pit of my stomach.

So when the mountain infantry soon came to get me—saying I'd abused the people's hospitality by leaving my designated lodgings, and so they would have to revoke my permit and ban me forever from the Sinistra Zone—I hadn't even gotten to sleep yet. Like a sentry I'd been long been alert, waiting for morning, waiting to finally be able to leave this place.

Parked nearby in the frosty nighttime was my jeep, with Géza Kökény himself, like a statue, watching over it.

The shortest route toward Greece led once again over the

Baba Rotunda Pass. In the dead of night, against the silence of the setting moon, I arrived at the top. Even now, I saw my ski tracks winding their way in a silver ribbon over those meadows toward the subterranean streams of the Kolinda forest. One last time a pleasant little warmth came over me there, in the Sinistra Zone: I wouldn't vanish from here without a trace, after all.